THE LADY'S DEFIANCE

The Royal Court Series

ANNE R BAILEY

Inkblot Press

For my love

You can also follow the author at: www.inkblotpressco.ca

FOREWORD

In an effort to avoid confusion because of their similar names I refer to Mary Howard and Mary Shelton as cousins in this book. However, they were only distantly related (though the Sheltons were considered part of the Howard faction at court).

As always while I mention real events and people this is a work of fiction. Names, characters, places and incidents either are the product of the author's imagination or are used fictitiously.

CHAPTER 1

Her hand moved past the cream bodice with its square neckline and piped gold velvet to the crimson silk beneath. The fabric slid over her fingertips. Red had always been her colour.

"You may borrow my necklace for the occasion," her mother said, holding up the heavy piece to let the sapphires framed by brilliant pearls catch the light. "Your father didn't get his claws on everything I own."

"It won't match," Mary Howard said, her tone impetuous as she pulled out the crimson bodice from the pile before her. Mary watched her mother swing herself around to face her, wondering how she maintained her balance with that heavy box on her head. Unlike most of the fashionable women of the court, she continued to insist on wearing the old-fashioned gable hood.

"What do you mean?" Her mother spoke in that

soft yet stern way of hers that terrified the servants. They never knew if she was about to order them flogged in the courtyard or simply forgive them for a misstep.

Mary shrugged and said as nonchalantly as possible, "I will wear the red."

"You would look ridiculous standing at the altar, clashing with your husband's blue and cream," her mother said through gritted teeth.

Mary tossed her head back as though she didn't give a fig what he or her mother thought.

Long before this moment, Mary had stopped fearing her mother's temper. She had no power over her, not since they caught her smuggling letters in orange crates to the exiled dowager princess. Watching her open and close her mouth like some furious fish gasping for air, it was clear that she was aware of this too.

Her mother, the stout Elizabeth Stafford, daughter of the treasonous Duke of Buckingham, composed herself and turned a scrutinising eye on her.

"It is embarrassing enough that your father has agreed to this wedding in the first place. I shall not have you bring further shame upon me." Her gaze was dark and terrifying. Her stance proud. No one could ever forget she was descended from royal blood. Not that she would let them. Even her father's downfall had failed to teach her humility.

If her mother had ever shown her any affection,

Mary might have backed down. Instead she continued to defy her, something that clearly confounded her mother.

Mary would have pitied her, but she had made her choice. Her mother had sided with Katherine of Aragon during the king's divorce. Once she was forbidden from doing so openly, she switched to more covert methods. Her actions were unsurprising, seeing as Elizabeth Stafford had always been an outspoken defender of the old ways in fashion, politics, and religion.

This must have slipped her husband's mind during the years he worked to put Anne Boleyn on the throne. The Duke of Norfolk, always in such control, never thought his own wife would try to thwart all his ambitions and carefully laid-out plans. His wife's treasonous actions could've cast suspicion over the entire family. He feared that everything he had worked to build would crumble around him.

But the king was gracious. Nor did he execute her for treason like her father before her. Instead, he devised a crueller punishment and put her under house arrest with her husband as her jailor.

Once upon a time, her father had loved the strong-willed Elizabeth, but that affection had curdled into hatred by the time Mary had been out of swaddling bands. Their tempestuous fights were still famous throughout the kingdom.

"Father has plans for me," Mary said, letting her

contempt seep through with every word. "Not that you would know of them."

Her mother laughed. "Is it his plan? Or is he still dancing to the tune of that commoner?"

Mary took a step back, recoiling from her mother's dangerous words. She cast a sidelong look toward the servants waiting nearby. It was impossible they had not heard. Her mother had been vague, but Mary didn't think Anne Boleyn would see it that way.

"Let me know if you are planning on talking yourself into an early grave. I'd prefer to not be around to watch you do it." The frosty words had the desired effect of cooling her mother's temper. A flash of something passed over her mother's face as she regarded her. Her brows unfurled.

"Mary..." she began.

But Mary could feel her own frustration and anger bubble to the surface. She wanted to leave this room before she said something she would regret. "You will excuse me, Lady Mother," she said, leaving without another word.

She walked down the halls of Greenwich, composing herself as she went. She slipped into her father's rooms unannounced. Here, in these heavily draped rooms, the familiar smell of ink and parchment permeated the air. The Duke of Norfolk was never idle for long. A cursory glance around the room told her he was sitting in council. The door to her father's study was closed with two Howard guards stationed at the entrance. Mary took a seat on a stool near the fireplace. As she held her hands out toward the flames she saw how they trembled. A combination of nerves and cold coursing through her.

When she had been told she would be marrying Henry Fitzroy, the king's by-blow, she had wanted nothing more than to have her mother at her side. Now she wondered how she could ever have forgotten that her mother had never provided her with love, only danger.

She wasn't left to ponder her folly in silence for long.

The door to the study opened and out strode Charles Brandon, the Duke of Suffolk, looking mighty pleased with himself.

Mary couldn't help but recall what Mary Shelton had told her: the duke's new bride lived in terror of him.

"It's not that he's unkind, but he never gives her a moment's peace," Mary Shelton had whispered in her ear.

Mary had laughed. But now that it was her turn, she didn't know how she felt about a man pestering her with attention night and day.

The duke had spotted her and gave her a polite nod and smile. Long ago, he had been renowned as a great jouster. Handsome and tall, he had been the king's best friend. He had lost all of these attributes expect for the last. Looking at him now, Mary couldn't see what had dazzled the court so much. In his forties he had grown fat, and the thick beard he insisted on wearing made him look more like a wild bear than a dashing knight.

Mary took note of the five other gentlemen that strode out of the study. Then at last her father. When his gaze fell on her, she curtsied low as she ought to and waited. He beckoned her to come to him with a crook of his finger.

She bobbed another curtsy, taking the opportunity to take a peek in the room behind him. Papers were piled up on the large oak table. Her brother, Henry, the Earl of Surrey, was there. With the meeting over he seemed content to stretch out his legs by placing his muddied boots on the table.

"I see it only took a few moments, then?"

She looked up to see her father's sardonic smile.

She blinked. "If you are referring to my mother, then yes, my lord," she said. "She is being insufferable." Knowing any criticism of her would win his approval.

"Then she's just the same. I did warn you. Come in," he said, retreating back into the room.

She followed hot on his heels, wondering why she had not listened to him. Oh well.

She took a freshly vacated seat. Her father, leaning back in his seat at the head of the table, studied her.

"What do you have to say?"

"Mother doesn't approve of the match, in case her last letter left you in any doubt, and she still insists on being rude to the queen."

His eyebrow arched, but he wasn't surprised. "We will never break her of that habit, I'm afraid."

"You would if you let the king throw her in the tower for a season or two." Henry spoke with such heartlessness and rudeness that even her father could not tolerate it.

"Son, you shall learn to hold your tongue or I will have it cut out." He was riffling through some papers and then, finding what he was looking for, handed it to Mary. "I have not forgotten you wanted to see this."

She looked down to see a draft of a marriage contract laid out before her. It was her own. She had been desperate to see it. Her father had expected tears or protests. But instead she had asked for two things: to see the contract and to have her mother by her side.

Her eyes swept through the document. It contained provisions made for her death, her husband's death, any surviving heirs they might have, or if they both died without heirs. On and on it went, every possibility imaginable spread out before her. Such talks might have put off other people, but she read each line with cold calculation. She focused on what her jointure would be during her lifetime, what she would be entitled to as his widow, and what would pass on to her children, should there be any. She didn't particularly care what would happen to her dowry if she predeceased him. Though she bet her father would attempt to get it back. He did not like parting with Howard lands or Howard gold.

"Don't be too eager to count your coin if he should die," Henry said with a scoff. "The king has forbidden the two of you from living together as man and wife. Until you are older anyway."

She looked up from the document. That was new. Mary tried her best not to let her ignorance show.

"It would not matter. Once the contract is signed and sealed I would be his wife, in the eyes of the law and the sight of God."

"Don't try to be too clever, sister," Henry said, resting his chin on his palm. "There was just a court trial arguing against this very thing."

Mary clenched her jaw until the pain became unbearable. "I had not forgotten."

Her brother shrugged. "I was just trying to remind you. Seeing as you are always so busy running around with Shelton." He leaned forward. "Hopefully you have not followed her example."

Pressing her lips together, she leaned forward. "What example?" Daring him to speak.

Her brother had no shame and kept going. "Bedding every man in sight. You couldn't pass off some bastard child as Fitzroy's if you aren't even allowed to live together."

"Enough." Their father's command cut off any further conversation. "Henry, such talk is best left at the tavern rooms you frequent. Don't gape at me like that. Do you think it is a secret how you spend your time? You are my heir, but if you do not mend your ways I shall see to it that you never inherit. There are other Howards more apt for the role."

Mary watched with satisfaction as her brother bowed his head, sulking but not daring to say anything out loud. The Howard name was everything to their father. He would not tolerate a stain on their reputation. Others may not dream of disinheriting their wayward sons, but Mary believed her father wouldn't hesitate.

"As for you," her father said, turning to her. "You shouldn't egg on your brother. You know better than to prod a wild boar."

Mary couldn't help but laugh.

"It suits us as well for you and your husband to live apart," he said, musing. Mary didn't care one way or another, but people might think it was strange.

She didn't have time to dwell on it before he continued. "You could make a fresh marriage if this one was never consummated. If, of course, God forbid,"—her father paused to cross himself— "something should happen to the young duke. But in all likelihood this shall not come to pass. Let us toast that the pair of you shall grow old together and found a new Howard dynasty."

"They wouldn't be Howards," Henry muttered under his breath, but only Mary heard. He wasn't wrong.

Entering the queen's apartments was like stepping onto the stage of a great masque, except the actors were richly dressed and had impeccable pedigrees. They did not perform for common rewards like gold but rather for intangible power and influence. At the centre of all of this was her: Anne Boleyn.

Today she was dressed in a deep crimson dress hemmed with soft sable fur. Her dog, a small spaniel, chased a ribbon at her feet. She was busier watching it than the man reciting a sonnet he had composed. And no wonder. Mary, having heard the last two stanzas, could tell they were poorly done.

Sensing the new arrival, the queen's dark eyes rose to meet her own. Mary dropped into a low graceful curtsy and took her seat among the other unmarried maids-in-waiting. She wasn't keen to draw attention to herself, at least not today. If the queen was in a good mood, then she would be eager to tease her, and if not, her cruelty was equally unwanted.

They might be related, but that didn't mean anything to Anne Boleyn. On the surface, she represented the Howard faction at court. They had certainly benefited from her rise. But the truth was Anne looked out only for herself. In public, her father and her cousin presented a united front, but Mary had been witness to enough arguments that took place behind closed doors to know that it was all a facade. She wondered how much longer they could go on pretending.

"Here," a familiar voice said behind her.

Mary didn't have to look down to know the book pressed into her hand. The feel of the leather was as familiar to her as her own hand. "You added something?" she whispered back, curiosity nipping at her fingers to flip the cover over and see for herself. Not the smartest decision she could make given the secretive nature of her project. A moment later Mary had slipped the small leather-bound book into the pocket of her gown.

This book was her secret passion. She didn't need kisses and caresses; she needed words. Poetry, songs, all within reach. She had begun the project with Mary Shelton, her cousin by marriage. Mary considered herself a collector, and she knew she would never be satisfied. With Anne Boleyn on the throne there was a never-ending interest in poetry and scholarship. She would record it all. The leather-bound book had come to her one Christmas season blank, its crisp parchment hungry for ink. By now she couldn't remember how she had conceived the idea to copy down works she admired.

Lady Mary Shelton shuffled in closer as discreetly as possible. "A work by Nicholas Udall. Margaret got her hands on it."

Mary's eyebrows shot up in surprise. Margaret was Mary's younger sister by only a year. She could have been Mary's twin, but unlike her glowing plump sister, who turned heads as she walked past, she was quiet and reserved, more at peace in her rooms or praying in the chapel than attending to the queen or flirting with gentlemen.

"You know how she is. Always in the right place at the right time. No one notices her. By the way, she said she enjoyed your latest addition," Mary Shelton added in an undertone.

Mary inclined her head to let her cousin know she heard. The latest had been a poem of unknown origin. She would discover its author sooner or later. She had heard it performed by Mark Smeaton, but he lacked the talent to compose such beautiful verse himself. When she had questioned him, he had handed her a scrap piece of paper. The words barely legible in his thin scrawl.

Painstakingly, she had copied out the words, leaving room for the author's name at the bottom. It had circulated among her friends, and they had all approved of it.

"Have I missed anything?" she said, looking at Anne Boleyn, who was thanking the man for the sonnet with exaggerated praise.

"Nothing out of the usual. The king has not arrived yet," Mary Shelton said.

"Oh?" Mary leaned closer, eyes sparking with interest.

Her cousin shrugged. "He could have been delayed by something. He shuts himself up with Cromwell as often as anything else."

Mary hummed, but she wondered. "Maybe after all this time she's beginning to lose his favour." She regarded the queen with a more critical eye. She had never been a great beauty but had carried herself as though she was. Her confidence and intellect had always drawn men. Now, sitting on her large wingback chair, she looked strained.

"The French ambassador was also here." Mary Shelton liked to dole out news by the spoonful.

Mary's impatience must have been telling because she didn't have to ask what they said.

"He praised her to the skies and back," her cousin began, only to be interrupted by someone bumping into her. Anne's presence hall was packed today. "She interrupted him, asking why there had been no news from France about a betrothal for her daughter. The ambassador had been tight-lipped after that."

"And I'm guessing she didn't like that very much," Mary said, thinking of her cousin's temper.

Her cousin hid a laugh behind her hand and shook her head. No.

Anne Boleyn didn't tolerate anyone questioning her legitimacy. The old queen was still alive. She had fought tooth and nail to hold on to the throne. Even now, in her exile, she was insistent she was the true queen, despite waning support among the English.

While Katherine pleaded with her nephew, the Spanish emperor, for help, Anne was getting the king to pass laws. First to forsake the pope in Rome, then to proclaim her as the one true queen and to name her daughter, Elizabeth, his only legitimate heir. She was trying to reforge the world to suit her. But before Anne, there had been Katherine, and she had ruled for over twenty years.

As fickle as people were, they wouldn't forget. Even Mary could see that. Something must be clouding Anne's judgment, perhaps her anger or insecurity. Mary couldn't be sure. What she was sure of was that Anne, in her foolishness, was vocal about her fear of the old queen's power. She was so vehement in her belief that others began to believe in it too.

Katherine had been humiliated at every turn, her goods and lands stripped away, her daughter declared illegitimate, yet she remained resolute. Despite being nothing more than a prisoner, she still found the will to fight. She was becoming an inspiration to all those who could not tolerate this new England. And all thanks to her rival, Anne.

A herald came in to announce the king's arrival. Mary Shelton put a hand on her shoulder, indicating they would talk later.

Mary watched as the king strode in, a strained smile on his lips as he greeted his wife.

Anne invited him to sit by her side and he took the seat, but it wasn't her that his attention was focused on. His gaze travelled around the room, settling on a person here or there. Mary could see how he looked at Mary Shelton. A growing desire in his eyes. Anne did not take kindly to being ignored like this. She had begun chattering at a maddening pace.

Mary could make out most of the words. She was complaining about the French ambassador and Katherine, as always. The king nodded absentmindedly, but his gaze kept drifting away from his wife.

Then all of a sudden he got to his feet and asked if she wouldn't like to play cards.

She turned her dark gaze on him and gave him a nod.

Cards were brought out and they played a game. To Anne's dismay, he had chosen to play piquet. Two players materialised at the table. Lady Mary Shelton and Sir Francis Weston.

Mary watched with a grin of amusement as her pretty cousin played badly, losing all five pounds in one fell swoop. She sniffed and did her best to hold back tears. It was played beautifully. The king urged her to not cry.

"Perhaps she shouldn't play if she can't tolerate the losses," Anne said, her eyes sharp on Mary Shelton whenever the king wasn't looking her way.

"Not everyone has the wealth you have at your disposal," the king retorted. His eyes kept travelling back to Mary Shelton as if he couldn't help it.

Mary wondered what had made him so contrary to Anne this morning. She watched as he motioned for a page boy to approach. Not long after, as Anne finished shuffling the cards for a new game, the page returned with a small purse. He didn't bring it to the king but rather gave it to Mary Shelton with a bow.

Her cousin looked flustered and kept saying she couldn't accept. The king, warmed by her gratitude, gave her a patient smile. "Then consider it a loan, Lady Mary."

Mary looked away from the scene playing out before her to the courtiers standing around the chamber sharing glances and attempting to hide their smiles. Only George Boleyn, brother to the queen, wore a grim expression.

Mary followed the direction of his intense stare back to the card table where the spark of rage in the queen's black eyes was unmistakable.

It was perhaps worse for Anne Boleyn that neither the king nor Mary Shelton took notice. The queen was not known for being able to withhold her temper. So when she maintained her cool and dealt out the cards, Mary knew she must be planning some greater retribution. She felt compelled to say a silent prayer for Mary Shelton, sitting there seemingly oblivious to anyone but the king.

Mary would not trade places with her cousin for the world.

Later, in the relative privacy of the room they shared, Mary reprimanded Mary Shelton.

"What on earth were you thinking?"

Her cousin was plaiting her hair on the edge of her

bed, looking pleased with herself. "I was thinking it might be nice to have someone take notice of me."

Mary snorted. "Let's pretend you are right. You know what the queen is like. I can't imagine why you would want to flirt with her husband right in front of her."

Her cousin stopped her movements, considering her for a moment, then merely shrugged. Mary knew her well enough to know she was hiding something.

"He favours me. I wouldn't say no to a few gifts, maybe a wealthy husband once he tires of me."

"You speak as though you would become his mistress." Mary shuddered at the thought. He was not the attractive man he had been even three years ago. She could not see what appealed to her cousin.

"You're ignoring the fact that this is the king we are talking about. Think of the power and wealth at his disposal," Mary Shelton said, guessing what she was thinking.

"Blame my romantic sensibilities then for not having considered you were chasing after that."

Again her cousin looked away. A growing suspicion made Mary want to ask what was on her mind, but fear stopped her. Maybe she wouldn't like the answer.

She pulled out her notebook and read aloud the newest addition.

"It's wonderfully put. Rather tragic," she said after

taking a moment to catch her breath. "You don't know who wrote it?"

Mary Shelton shook her head. "It was passed along to me."

Mary studied the page, enjoying the rhythmic flow and turn of phrase. She glanced at her cousin and spotted her amused expression.

"Tell me the truth. How did you come across this?"

It didn't take much more prodding to get Mary Shelton to tell her the whole story.

"Weston recited it to me. Claiming it was his, but considering he rhymed 'heart' with 'cart' in his last performance, I called his bluff. He admitted he paid someone to write it for him. I thought it was good enough to be a part of your little project."

Mary's grin turned into a wide smile. "After a story like that, of course I give it my official seal of approval. We shall have to endeavour to discover the true author."

Mary Shelton sprang to her feet. "Enough of poetry. What about you? Are you excited for your wedding day? You shall be a duchess!"

Mary managed a shrug. She was tired of thinking about her wedding day. The event was marred by her parents, who seemed to be butting heads over everything.

"It will be a day like any other and nothing in my life will change."

A playful grin spread across Mary Shelton's

features. "Quite the contrary. You got the very best out of this arrangement. Just think Mary, you will have the title and his great fortune at your disposal in exchange for nothing. You don't even need to bed him."

Mary looked away. It was true she wasn't desperate to bed her husband-to-be. His tall yet lanky appearance and turned-up nose didn't inspire love or devotion in her. He wasn't handsome enough to tempt her into sinful thoughts. The poems in her books spoke of burning love and affection. She doubted he could invoke such emotions in her. On the other hand, instead of becoming a woman she was forced to stay a child, living in her father's house. She had dreamed of the independence that would come with her marriage, but that dream was washed away.

"Well, it could be worse," Mary Shelton reminded her, sitting down next to her and patting her hands. "Maybe you will be allowed to remain at court and then what fun we will have." Then her face grew grave. "Mary, you must promise me something."

"What?"

"If you are given rooms of your own, you must let me stay with you."

The two women convulsed into fits of laughter.

"I swear, I swear," Mary said, wiping tears from her eyes.

CHAPTER 2

Their wedding was a simple affair held in the queen's chapel. Considering it had been good enough for the king and Anne Boleyn, Mary could hardly complain about the cramped room and the haste with which it was done.

Her mother had been packed away back to one of her father's many estates. They hadn't spoken again and Mary was relieved she was gone. She didn't wish to think of her and her selfishness anymore.

She would smile until she forgot that her mother had laughed and called her a puppet.

By the time she walked through the double doors of the great hall on the arm of her husband, she was beaming.

There was a banquet thrown in their honour. Most of the court attended. In any other situation she would have been honoured, but she was forced to sit beside her new husband for the entire duration.

It dragged on and on and she couldn't even dance.

He began to irritate her with his impetuous behaviour. She knew most of the courtiers had always referred to him as the little princeling and she could see why. He did resemble his father in the set of his mouth and his beady little eyes, but he wasn't chivalrous as the king was said to be. Instead, he acted like a child, rude to the servants and haughty to everyone else. It took every fibre of her being to keep the smile on her face and not let her annoyance show.

At her side, her husband was having more trouble with this. He kept casting looks her way. The tilt of his head told her that he was appraising her. She didn't give him the satisfaction of letting her discomfort show.

Unlike other women at court, she knew her value down to the last penny. If anything, she was too good for him.

They were watching a performance of acrobats. They twirled and leapt through the air, and the courtiers applauded. It was around this time Mary felt his hand creep over hers.

And at last she was forced to look his way.

"Yes, my lord?" She turned a steely gaze to him.

His surprise was plain on his face. He had not been expecting her to react like this. He cleared his throat.

"I have been told this is to be a marriage in name only."

"I know." She was bored. She wanted to pull her hand away from his sweaty grip, but that might be seen as weakness.

"There are ways...you are my wife. It would not be improper."

She flashed him a toothy grin. "It would be to disobey the king. Something I dare not do." She paused. "Even for my husband."

His lips, already thin, disappeared as he pursed his mouth.

"From what I heard, it is your health that the whole kingdom is concerned about. They wouldn't wish you to exert yourself over me."

He leaned closer to her so they wouldn't be overheard, but he spoke loudly all the same.

"I am a man! Strong and virile like my father. Are you suggesting otherwise?"

For a second the grip on her hand tightened.

She was sure everyone had heard him. She caught a few people nearby glance their way. She wondered what madness possessed her to aggravate her new husband like this, but something drove her onward.

"It is not me who is suggesting it but rather your own father. I have no say in the matter. None of this"—she waved her free hand around to indicate the room—"was my idea. So please direct your complaints to someone who would help you."

"You don't wish to be married to me?" He let her hand go. This time she had genuinely shocked him.

"My opinion does not matter."

A sidelong glance at him allowed her to see a myriad of emotions swimming across his face. Surprise, insult, anger, disappointment. She considered that until this moment, perhaps he had cherished the illusion that he was a handsome princeling everyone was fawning over. She wondered what could have made him believe that.

He did not speak for a long time, so she returned her attention to the wafer placed before her.

The sugar dissolved in her mouth, and she caught the notes of raspberries and rosewater. Delicious.

"Did no one tell you which colours I would be wearing today?" he all but spat.

"They did." She dabbed the corner of her lips with a kerchief. "I preferred to wear this gown instead. Does it displease you?"

She spoke so demurely that he couldn't fault her. All the same, his eyes narrowed.

"Your brother said you were a wildcat. Well, I for one am glad that I shall not have to put up with your company for long." He added the last bit as a parting shot, but given that she didn't care about gaining his favour, she merely shrugged. She was surprised to hear that he had spoken to her brother. Henry was never at court these days, preferring to carouse in the country on his own estates, but he was also an opportunist. Of course he would find a way to ingratiate himself with the person who might one day be king.

It was why her father had even agreed to the union. Otherwise, a bastard son, even if he came from royal lineage, was hardly a suitable match for a Howard.

She decided it would be in her best interest to mollify him. He was still a child in many respects, despite his claims to the contrary.

"You will find I am a good wife to you. Even if we are not allowed to live together as man and wife. I made my vows at the altar and I intend to keep them." She let out a sigh. "I hope we shall come to an understanding."

He liked this, as she guessed he might.

Thankfully, he didn't talk to her for the rest of the banquet. After they were congratulated by the king and queen, off they went back to their respective lives. This was a mere blip in Mary's day-to-day routine. The only difference was that now everyone called her "Your Grace."

※

"You shall return to the country and that is final."

Mary was trying to keep her body from shaking. "That is the last thing I wish to do. What business is there for me in the country?"

"What business is there for you here?" her father shot back at her.

"We were to live apart." Mary couldn't help the whine in her voice.

"Yes, but that does not preclude you from playing the part of a good wife," he said. "You shall have a household to manage and maybe one day even more. But enough of that. You will go where I send you."

Mary crossed her arms in front of her. "My husband might not wish me to leave court. Should it not be him that dictates where I go?"

Her father laughed. "I swear, if you were not my daughter…"

But Mary could see that, despite his humour, she was coming close to crossing a line with him. She knew by the glint of fury in her father's eyes that she wouldn't be able to make him budge on this.

"If you wish to debate this, then let me lay out my reasons. I have taken young Fitzroy in as my ward. So my authority over you is higher than his. He is in the country staying with your brother. You shall travel to my estates and learn to manage a household. You have no business at court, but overseeing your husband's lands might be something you could put your mind to."

Mary knew it was a sign of her father's affection for her that he even bothered explaining this to her. Still, she would rather remain here. Much more exciting things were happening at court. What poetry could be found among the farmers and tenants of her father's lands?

"How long?" she whispered, desperate to know.

"I think you shall return for Christmas. Cheer up. You know I cannot tolerate tears."

"I am not crying," she said scowling. "When have I ever cried? You will excuse me. I suppose I shall have to start packing."

She bowed to him and fled the room. She did her best to keep her composure calm. Inside, her emotions were battling. She was proud her father was entrusting her with so much responsibility. After all, when he had made this marriage for her, he had done it with the hope that he might one day see her on the throne. She should be grateful, but...

She was also upset. When would she have a say in where she went and what she did?

She wanted to be here. Mary thought of her friends, her poetry, at the forefront of it being here to witness the machinations of the court. Listening to the readings and developments going on around her. She couldn't bring herself to jump for joy at the prospect of the quiet country where there was no place for poetry and debate.

She was going about her business packing away her letters and personal possessions herself when Mary Shelton came into the room.

"I take it you haven't been given apartments of your own at court."

"No." Mary's tone was sour. She regarded her cousin, unable to keep the envy from bubbling up to the surface. She had always strived to be the perfect daughter. To represent the Howards. Yet here was her cousin, a shameless flirt and purposefully ignorant to the world, rewarded. "Unlike some, I apparently am not allowed to stay here."

Mary Shelton's cheerful smile vanished. "Where are you going?"

"My father's house. I'll be in Norfolk while you are here flirting with every handsome man. Inspiring countless more poems." She let out a heavy sigh.

"I wouldn't mind going with you." Mary Shelton placed a hand on her shoulder. Her touch was light, as if she was approaching a wary animal.

"So come, then. I certainly have room for you in my train, and my father's house is empty most of the time anyway."

Mary Shelton held her gaze for a moment before she shook her head slowly. "I cannot."

"Why?"

"I am ordered to stay at court."

Mary could see her cousin trying to force herself to smile. She failed miserably. A twinge of guilt filled her.

"I thought you loved it here. So many interesting people..."

Mary Shelton chuckled. "You sure know how to turn a phrase. But...my life is not my own either. I am not as free as you think I am."

Mary bit the inside of her cheek. Mary Shelton was begging her to ask. She looked eager to share a secret. The temptation to ask was great, but she hesitated and tried to distract her with another topic.

"Has the queen spoken to you yet?"

"Oh, she tried to see if I could be sent from court. But she failed. But at least she knows I'm not a risk to her. The family has made her see that she needs me around."

Finally, unable to bear it any longer, Mary asked, "What is going on? Why would she need you around? Tell me, or let me think the worst of you."

Mary had straightened up and faced her cousin, taking her two hands in hers so she could not run. "We must tell each other the truth. There can't be lies between friends."

"I've been commanded by my family to be here to distract the king. If the queen goes into confinement again, I am to be there if he should go looking for a..." Her cousin struggled with the word. "Mistress."

"No." Mary was gaping. "I thought you were chasing after him for his favour, for the challenge. Or for trinkets and gold..."

"Is that how little you think of me?"

A pair of servants came into the room. Mary cleared her throat. They looked to her for guidance on what should be taken to the carts next. It was a while before she could turn back to her pretty cousin.

"I'm sorry, but you always had a knack for flirtation. I simply thought the king intrigued you."

Mary Shelton leaned closer to her. "Would you be intrigued by him?"

Mary smiled. "He is my father-in-law. How could I answer that? I am not a Seymour at Wolfhall."

They laughed. The court had been agog at the scandal that came from the Seymours. Such a small family whose bloodline went far back to the days of the Normans should have been forgotten by everyone. The eldest daughter, Jane, was lucky to have even been given a place at court. Lord knew they could barely afford the expense of keeping her dressed properly. The other ladies in the queen's household always commented on her dowdy appearance.

"Pretend you are, then," Mary Shelton said, a mischievous glint in her eyes. Her dark mood had gone. She never could stay sad for very long.

"Then no, I would not be—intrigued by him," Mary confirmed. They were speaking in such vague terms that even if someone had overheard them there would be nothing for them to report. "You don't have to do this. Or you could make sure you fail miserably at your task."

Mary Shelton nodded. "I know, but in a way you are right. This is a challenge. This is my chance to become something greater than I am. Who knows, I might make a fabulous match far above my station— just like Bessie Blount did. Or maybe I will be given a tidy fortune."

"A manor or two would be nice. Something you couldn't lose gambling away at the next card game," Mary teased.

"I do have a weakness for gambling." Mary Shelton looked around at the now sparse room. "I'll miss you."

"I shouldn't be gone for too long. But you will have to keep your ears to the ground for me. Send any new additions my way, please."

"Have you ever thought of taking up the pen yourself?"

"No, I am a curator. I cannot write poetry."

"You will have plenty of time to practice."

A groan escaped her. A wave of fresh dread overtaking her. "I didn't think my marriage would leave me worse off. On the other hand, in the country I will be on my own with no one telling me how I should be spending my day."

"You will be using all your money to purchase parchment and ink," Mary Shelton predicted.

"Wouldn't be such a bad thing to spend my fortune on."

"And when your father finds out, he can use it as kindling for your pyre. In the long run it's a very economical purchase."

"I hadn't thought of that. But it's the sort of considerate thing I would do," Mary said with a barely contained smile. Then she turned serious. "Mary, I can try to do something for you if you are really unhappy. I don't wish to see you..."

"Don't worry about me." Her cousin flashed her a pretty smile. "I am happy enough confiding my troubles to you."

"I hope I am the only one you confide in. You

cannot let anyone know of this. Our enemies would jump at the chance to discredit us with the king."

"Our enemies?"

Mary was confused by the question. "Yes. The enemies of all Howards. Not everyone is pleased we have risen so high. Even before Anne was made queen we were a powerful family."

"But you aren't a Howard anymore," Mary Shelton pointed out. A dryness to her tone.

Mary gaped at her. "No..." she started slowly. "But they are my family. My affinity."

"This could have been your chance to escape it all."

Mary finally got what she was alluding to. "Unfortunately," she said, running a hand over her embroidered stomacher, "I don't have the option. I think if I ever showed signs of disobedience, my father..."

"You love him, yet you fear him just as much."

A shrug was all Mary could manage. Her emotions were hard to put into words.

"I am his daughter," she said, as if that would explain everything.

She didn't want to think about this. Mary Shelton had come here to keep her company as she packed, not to have a lengthy conversation.

"At this rate, I'll never be able to finish getting my things in order."

Mary Shelton swept a glance around the room. "I

think you could manage. If you forget anything, I'll send it to you."

჻

The road toward Kenninghall was dreary. The weather alternated between pouring rain and overcast skies.

Only the comforting thought that she wouldn't be travelling to Sheriff Hutton, where her husband was, nor to her mother at Redbourn kept her from disobeying her father and turning back around.

Her escort took refuge at every great house they could. They were so covered in mud that many took a second look at them before granting them hospitality. She wasn't surprised. After all, they looked more like ruffians than the retinue of a royal duchess.

Each night Mary spent a good part of it scrubbing the mud and grime from her face and hair. Even this was not enough, but she had given up looking presentable.

She dreamed of a hot bath to soothe the flea bites on her back and even contemplated cutting her hair. It now itched with lice, even though her maid took pains to comb her hair. She tried to put on a brave face. She tried to remember that many had it worse than her. For some this was their everyday reality.

At last their misery came to an end. She could see Kenninghall and its surrounding fields and buildings. For the first time since they began their trip she felt relief. Even her mare's ears pricked forward, as if she knew they were home and that oats and a dry stable awaited her.

Mary set a gruelling pace, but no one minded. They all wanted this journey to be over.

"These are to be your new rooms, Your Grace," her father's steward said with a bow as he pushed open the heavy wooden door.

She had been moved to quarters that benefited her new status. If this were any other time, she would have explored her new living quarters, taking stock of everything she owned. But being inside Kenninghall's pristine walls just reminded her of how filthy she was.

She walked through her privy chamber to the door that led to an inner chamber. A fire was blazing in the hearth. To her relief, a basin was already being filled with buckets of hot water.

"I suspected you might wish to bathe upon arrival. The weather has been terribly foul. Apologies if I overstepped." As he spoke he kept his eyes demurely low.

Mary smiled at the deference. How she had risen in the world. "No. Thank you. It is just what I was looking forward to."

"Then I shall leave you to your maids. Will you be dining in the hall tonight?"

"In my room. I doubt I shall be presentable to be

put on display," she rambled, but he nodded politely and with another bow left.

It paid to have good servants and her father always hired the very best. His retainers never left their posts if they could help it. He paid the best, rewarded hard work, and made sure his men had the very best. If she were a man with a trade or skill, she would go knocking on a Howard's door.

Luckily, she didn't have to.

She had been born a Howard and was now a duchess.

For the first time since her wedding this fact truly sank in.

At official court functions she would wear ermine like her father. If it was true what they whispered behind the queen's back, then the king might have her husband named as his legal heir, which would make her the future queen of England.

The thought made her shake.

"More water, my lady?"

Her maid jumped to her feet. Mary shook her head. The water was still warm. Her skin was glowing pink from the earlier heat. She took a sponge and scrubbed herself raw.

Her hair was washed and her maid brushed scented oil through it.

Already Mary felt more like herself. She slipped into a clean shift and threw a heavy furred mantle on top.

Her supper was laid out on a table with a cup of mulled wine beside a thick stew. Her curiosity won over her hunger.

She wanted to explore first.

One door from her inner chamber led to her bedchamber. A large four-poster bed had been made ready for her with all the trappings a duchess should have. New tapestries she had not seen before also covered the walls in here. It was altogether promising.

From the window she could see one of the inner courtyards and the gatehouse of Kenninghall. Her maid had a chamber of her own adjoining hers. The second door led to a closet, a prie-dieu already installed for her, and then the third door, which could be hidden behind a tapestry, was a long gallery. For the moment it was empty, but Mary already envisioned that she could turn this into a room to store all her gowns and possessions.

It was pointless to think of the future with her husband. Perhaps one day they might live together in a house, but that day was long in coming. In the meantime, she would set herself up.

She returned to her inner chamber to eat before praying and retiring for the night. Tomorrow would be a fresh new day.

Mary settled into life at Kenninghall with all the ease of a hawk returning to its perch in the mews. She did it out of habit rather than enjoying it. This was the role she had been trained to perform: the obedient daughter. She didn't think she would deviate from that anytime soon.

She was glad to have been allotted such big apartments. She could comfortably spend the day in her rooms if she wished. Especially now that her writing desk had been brought in.

After mass, she would go for an early morning ride before breaking her fast. When the sun was unbearable, she would sit and work on some needlework, something she had always been deft at, or take up the lute. After eating a meal in the great hall for all the tenants and local landowners to come gawk at her, she would retire to her privy chambers and would spend time at her writing desk until her eyes began stinging.

Kenninghall was not quite as empty as her father had made it sound. First of all, the Howard family was large and prolific, but not all had tidy fortunes and estates of their own. As one of her father's more glamorous houses, Kenninghall was never without visitors for long.

Some had been assigned permanent apartments in the house or on the extensive grounds. The most notable was her uncle, another Thomas Howard, who lived in a little hunting lodge within sight of the main house. He was nothing like her father in both age and disposition. Being only twenty-two and full of optimism, he was the embodiment of chivalry. He had spent much of his childhood studying in France and then fought in the king's army against the Scots.

She had never seen much of him until this year when he had travelled to London to witness Anne Boleyn's coronation and everyone had been impressed by his charming conversation.

Mary suspected it wouldn't be long before her father found a way to capitalise on his budding popularity. But for now her uncle had been packed away to the country. Just like her.

The other notable resident at Kenninghall was her father's mistress. Elizabeth, or Lady Bess as the servants called her, had been installed here years ago. She had taken over the apartments that used to belong to the duchess. Mary had no idea what she did all day but didn't trouble herself to find out.

Despite all the honours heaped on her, Bess knew her place. She did not come traipsing into the great hall trying to play the part of the duchess. She kept out of the way unless her father was in residence. Mary was sure she would have hated her if it were not for this.

She saw more of the household steward and the groom in the stable than anyone else until one day she heard the sound of cantering hooves approaching the courtyard.

She shielded her eyes from the glaring sun, just in

time to see the great warhorse her uncle rode come charging in.

He smiled to see her, not at all surprised to find her here.

"Good morning, Your Grace," he said with a respectful tilt of his head. "I thought I might join you today."

Mary hid her surprise. "You are welcome to do so." She indicated to her ladies. "We shall not be hunting today."

"I know." He flashed her a quick smile before hopping down from the saddle in one fluid motion. "I spoke with your page. Besides, I can see you aren't prepared for a hunt."

"I didn't want you to be disappointed." She was on uneasy ground. She could hear the whisper of voices from her ladies behind her. She frowned as she thought she caught a giggle.

"Well, you may join us, then," she said with a sniff. She got into the saddle with practiced ease.

"Thank you." He doffed his cap and with a wink to one of her ladies-in-waiting behind her hopped back into the saddle himself.

They set off, his horse keeping pace with her mare though it looked eager to outpace her. She kept wondering what had led to his sudden appearance. She had been at Kenninghall for a few weeks now and he had never thought to speak to her before. She didn't think she had even been in the same room as him until now.

Curiosity made her slow the pace so that they might talk. For the first time she was able to study him. She had to admire his horsemanship, and the way he carried himself would leave no one in doubt that he was a Howard. It was a shame that he had become obsolete. He was a younger son of a former duke. Nothing more. The thought was cruel and she was ashamed it had even popped into her head.

"I was surprised to hear your name brought up by my friends," he said, without turning his head. "I was even more surprised to discover that my brother's child was interested in something like poetry. Your friends send anything good your way, don't they?"

She bit the inside of her cheek to keep herself from swearing. "I am surprised my name is brought up at all. Who are these friends?" Neither confirming nor denying he was right.

He ignored her question like she had his.

"Not to worry, I'll keep your secret safe. My brother prefers to pretend I don't exist, and he wouldn't appreciate me coming to him with gossip. Not about his little duchess."

Mary saw a flicker of emotion cross his face before his smile returned and he continued. "Besides, I rather approve of your activities and I'm even more curious to have a look at your collection."

"Why should I let you see it, now that you have sworn not to tell my father?" she pointed out.

"A true courtier's answer, but then you must know that I could be lying or change my mind." His tone was matter-of-fact. Then with a laugh he added, "And now that you've admitted you are keeping poems stashed away—well, I could order your rooms searched. I am still the elder and a worried uncle looking out for the well-being of his niece."

If it wasn't for his easy manner and sarcasm, she would've been panicking. She reminded herself there was nothing wrong with what she was doing. Her father disliked poetry, but why should that worry her? She kept it hidden to avoid all the fuss and scrutiny. He'd probably huff and puff, but after a while he'd forgive and forget. He always did. At least when it came to her.

"There's no danger in a bit of poetry." She dug her heels into the horse's side, spurring her onward.

"Then you haven't been paying attention," he called after her. If he said anything further, she didn't hear. Now all she wanted to do was to forget everything, enjoy her ride. All the anxieties that had come bubbling to the surface were to be suppressed. She was a Howard. Howards weren't weak and they didn't hide.

By the time they returned to the house, she felt like herself once more.

That evening, he joined her to dine in the great hall and she did her best to make him feel welcome.

"You ride well," he said. "I apologise if I upset you. It was not my intention."

"You threatened me," she said with a calm serenity in her voice. "Or failed to do so. If that is how you go about making friends, no wonder you've been tucked away in the country for so long."

He didn't reply but handed her a neatly sealed envelope.

"What is this?" she said, not touching it.

"You might enjoy it. It's a peace offering," he said with a tilt of his head toward her. "We Howards forget how to play nicely with others. There are rumours we eat our own young, and the older I get the more I am certain it is true."

"Well, at least some of us can admit when we are wrong. It means there is hope for us." She laughed. "And as much as I tease you, as you can see, I too have been sent away to the country. Until I am needed again. So I am no less free than you."

He wiped his hands on a cloth napkin and motioned the server over with the crook of his finger. "Bring me something stronger than this wine."

The man nodded and disappeared.

"You will either get used to it or find a way to carve your own path."

He looked weary as he spoke, looking far older

than his age, but he lost all resemblance to her father. He never looked weary.

"At least we do all this waiting and figuring out our life in one of the greatest houses in England," she said.

"True, I should be grateful. You are wise for your years."

At the centre of the hall a travelling musician strung up his lute and cleared his throat. She had paid for him to perform this evening. In this moment, sitting at the high table underneath the canopy of estate, she felt very much like a great lady.

"You don't know me at all, Lord Uncle." Her smile grew wider. Her gaze fixed on the lute strings, the ghost of a song already filled her mind.

CHAPTER 3

"The chambers and parlours glittered,
Bay windows, as fine as ever there were.
The galleries—warm—invited every
    sort,
Dancing and wisdom flowed through
    the halls.
You would think it the promised
    paradise,
If it were not for the gilded bars."

Mary read the last of the poem out loud for her ladies. It was simple and short, but she enjoyed it.

"Pretty, but I didn't see any gilded bars on his hunting lodge," Agnes Ingleby said before giggling.

"And when did you see his hunting lodge?" Joyce Carre called her bluff.

Mary didn't mind them teasing each other. They could daydream about love as much as they wanted as long as it went no further than words. Despite her age and interests, she wouldn't tolerate a household filled with flirtation and scandal. She had too much pride in her own reputation to allow it to be dragged through the mud.

But this was nothing. She let them have their fun and instead focused on the thin sheet of paper in her hand.

Her uncle surprised her. This was the latest poem he had shared with her. Over the last few weeks he had shared many others, including some that others had composed—those mysterious friends of his.

As if she had summoned him, the doors to her presence chamber opened and the usher announced Lord Thomas Howard.

Her ladies' conversation turned to laughter. She could just imagine Agnes turning red.

"Have I interrupted something?" he asked, looking from one lady to another.

"I just finished reciting your latest poem," Mary said.

He looked at her ladies with mock hurt. "And my words are the cause of such amusement. It must have been a very terrible poem."

A chorus of "no's" followed his comments.

He held up his hands. "Peace, I was teasing. But I thought I would join you ladies today for a while. The weather has taken a turn for the worst, and I am afraid I have had to cancel my hunting excursion."

"What a shame," Joyce said with a giggle.

Mary rolled her eyes, but she turned her attention to her uncle.

She moved toward her desk, where she kept her notebook tucked away in a secret compartment under lock and key. "Agnes, why don't you play the lute for our visitor? Joyce, you can sing."

If any grumbled, Mary didn't pay attention. She sat at her desk and pulled out her book, motioning him over. "Will you give me permission to make a copy of this poem?"

He nodded. "I would be honoured."

He had a hungry look in his eyes as he regarded the notebook of hers.

She slid it over toward him. "Perhaps you would like to see the other work I have copied? You will find you are in good company."

He smiled. "I suppose a part of me fears that. But then I also live in terror that my work is not as good."

She leaned back. "You could always improve."

He took the book.

She watched him as he studied a few pages with all the seriousness of a scholar.

"This is very well done." He chuckled before adding, "You should start a university for poets. You are well on your way to becoming an expert and training lots of other professors alongside you."

"Thank you," she said. "I don't share my little hobby with many people."

"I know how many would feel about a daughter studying poetry," he admitted.

"And do you disapprove or think ill of me for it?"

He tilted his head. "No, but then you are not my daughter."

"It's silly to think anything untoward would happen from a bit of poetry."

"It's the language of love and scandal."

"And pain and angst," she interrupted. "Poetry doesn't have to be only about love. But debating it won't matter. We won't change people's opinions overnight. But when I left the court it had been a place of study, music, and learning. Poetry included. For all her faults and low birth others might criticise her for, Queen Anne has changed the court. It's no longer just prayer and sewing. We shall be as fashionable and educated as the French."

"You paint a pretty picture of the court, Lady Mary. Careful, I might begin to pine for it," he said. "I know that everyone is obsessed with the new learning. Out with the old and in with the new. I am teasing, but I am truly happy to hear that the court is changing for the better. Soon we shall be the envy of all of Europe."

"Were we ever not?" Mary teased but thought for a moment. "I suppose the years before the queen's ascension were filled with struggle and apprehension. The break with Rome and—" She stopped her train of thought. "Well, happier days lie ahead of us." She had been dangerously close to admitting to him more than she should.

Mary had been witness to her father's horror when the king declared that the pope was merely the bishop of Rome. Her father was an ambitious man, but even he had his limits. It had been a lot for him to swallow, and he hoped that once the threat of Spain was lifted and Anne was securely on the throne with a prince in the nursery, then Henry might make peace with the pope and return England to the Catholic fold. Few people knew of the threat of excommunication, but as a member of the privy council her father knew everything.

The reminder of this other more dangerous side of court made Mary reflect on her desire to return so quickly.

"I have been pleasantly surprised by Kenninghall," she said at last. She could see her uncle's mind had been drifting too.

"It's not such a bad place. You can make of it what you will," he pointed out. "Don't you have a large fortune at your disposal?"

Mary grinned. "This is true. We should throw pageants, have dance masters and musicians come in. We don't need to sulk around indoors."

Over the next few weeks Mary made an effort to make Kenninghall a livelier place that would suit her. She was using her own funds for the small improvements she made here and there, so she didn't think her father would mind.

The bowling green was cleaned and a roof was installed so they would be able to bowl even when it rained. The lead roof had been the most expensive addition.

She ordered a pavilion cleared away in the gardens so that she and her ladies might have little archery tournaments and invited dance masters from London to come teach them the new dances.

Every day they could find something fun to do.

One cloudy morning she found herself watching the sky for any signs of an impending storm. Her attention was diverted by a rider arriving in the courtyard.

She breathed a sigh of relief when she saw it was a messenger from Sir Ogden, one of her father's vassals. The feeling of relief surprised her. She used to stand in this very spot every morning hoping that today a message would arrive summoning her back to court. When was the last time she had done that? When had she changed her mind?

She thought wistfully that today she had been hoping to go hawking, but it was better not to take the risk of getting caught in the rain.

They would settle in for a quiet day in her rooms. Perhaps it was a sign, considering how behind she was on her needlework, and her embroidery projects had been abandoned for far too long.

She was threading thread in her needle when the gossip began.

Joyce had been practicing the steps of a dance with Constance, but Agnes, bored of reading psalms out loud, had begun to divulge all the news she had heard.

"I heard that asparagus has appeared on the queen's plate again."

"It's not the season for it," Joyce called out over the music.

Agnes shrugged. "Perhaps they were preserved. But you know what that means."

"There's been no official announcement yet," Mary said.

Agnes frowned. "Perhaps it's too soon, but they say the king has stopped visiting her rooms and that a pretty girl has caught his eye."

Mary put down her sewing. "Who?"

Agnes' shoulders slumped. "I don't know."

"Your sources can't be very good or accurate. If the king knows, then the whole court would know soon enough," Mary said, trying her best not to grind her teeth. She thought of Mary Shelton. Had she succeeded? Was she the king's new mistress now? It had been a few weeks since she had heard any news from her, so anything was possible. Her own sources had not told her about the queen. But everyone was hopeful and eager to make gossip out of nothing. She wouldn't countenance it until she heard more.

That evening as they ate, her uncle joined them dining in the great hall.

"I was thinking about that book of yours."

"Oh?" she said, picking at her mutton. She had lost her appetite.

"What if you were to circulate it around court? There are plenty who would wish to read it. That old poetry by Skelton is not readily found in many places."

"True, but I wouldn't wish to part with it. What if it gets lost?"

"Entirely possible. You could make a copy."

Mary's hand cramped just thinking about it. "I could let you do it," she teased. "I am very busy."

"Pay a clerk to do it. I am sure one of them would oblige you."

"Yes, and just as quickly go running off to my father." She paused. "Perhaps it wouldn't be the worst idea though."

"Yes, occasionally a brilliant thought does strike me."

"Have you written anything new?" she asked.

"I thought you might ask me if I have any news from court."

He was trying to encourage her to ask. In this moment he reminded her of Mary Shelton.

"Have you any news from court? I didn't think you would be a great source of knowledge on that score."

"Ouch, that stung," he said with a laugh. "But as it happens, this time I do have news. Some of which might intrigue you."

"Fine, I'll bite. Tell me." She turned to face him. "You have my full attention."

His wide grin told her at least that this was good news.

"We are to return to court earlier than expected. I am to come along too. My kind brother has found me a place in the king's household."

"Oh, that's wonderful!" she said. "When?"

"I assume your father will write to you soon. I suppose sometime within the next few weeks. Next time don't discount me."

She smiled. "Well, I mean you have such a reputation as a recluse. What did you want me to think?"

"I'm working on that. But as you know, it is not entirely by choice that I am here."

"No one told you to be the younger son of a great duke," she said, grinning. Her spirits lifted at the thought of reuniting with her friend.

But by the time she reached the privacy of her bedchamber she was less excited by the news. It was likely that the queen was pregnant and the Howards were to rally to her side. If she did have a boy this time, then they would be on hand to reap the rewards. But she had begun to build a life for herself here. Maybe she wasn't keen on returning. She definitely wasn't eager to be around Anne Boleyn day and night. Would her husband be at court too? Would she be forced to play the part of the good wife in this sham of a marriage? Or worse, what if the king said they should begin living together as man and wife?

Mary shivered at the thought. A feeling of dread rose within her. She could never tolerate how her mother had been exiled from her own home. What if her husband had similar plans for her? Would her father step in? Would he allow her to live at Kenning-hall? The uncertainty ate away at her confidence.

"Be calm. Be calm," she repeated to herself. But nothing worked. Finally, she picked up her notebook and read poetry out loud. Losing herself in the world of chivalrous love, adventure, comedy, and wit made her relax at last.

What would be would be.

"A messenger for you, my lady," the household steward said with a bow. "He's come from your father in London."

"Send him in," Mary said with a bow. She was looking for samples of fabric from the tailors in London. She had in mind a new gown for the Christmas season.

The man appeared travel-stained from the roads, but his expression wasn't grim. This must be the letter she was expecting.

She took it from his outstretched hand with a nod and tilt of her head in thanks.

She went over to her desk and broke the seal.

Her father wrote succinctly. She was to remain at Kenninghall until the last of the harvest was brought in. Then she was to travel to London with all haste.

She set down the letter. There was nothing there about her husband, what her father intended, or any news whatsoever.

The messenger was still waiting.

"I shall write a response to my father now. Will you be travelling back to him?" she asked.

"Yes, Your Grace."

"Then go eat and rest and I will have someone bring the letter to you." She gave him a smile, which he returned. "Is there any other news from court? How is the king? I trust he's in good health? And the queen as well?"

"Yes, they both are."

She watched his expression. Either he wouldn't say anything more or he didn't know. Her father was careful with who he hired. His men were well-trained and knew how to keep their mouths shut.

No one interrupted her as she dipped her pen in the ink. The letter was short, but she considered each word and took care to make sure her writing was neat and even. At the end she signed her name, adding the moniker "the Duchess of Richmond and Somerset."

While she waited for the ink to dry she pulled out

a fresh sheet of parchment. This she addressed to her cousin, Mary Shelton, asking for news.

Both letters were sealed and sent to the messenger with instructions. She only hoped she would be receiving a reply before long.

In the meantime she found herself itching to do something more than just occupy her time with pleasantries. She left her ladies to their amusements and accompanied the chamberlain to the record rooms of Kenninghall. Here ledgers and accounts were stored under lock and key. As the harvest was brought in and taxes collected, everything was written down in a book somewhere. Fair market value was calculated on each consignment of goods and expectation of income was determined for the following year. Other books held the costs of running a great household. Everything was accounted for. Nothing was too insignificant not to be kept track of.

She took up her pen, checking the sums and keeping a mental account of where the numbers should be. Was the estate burning away money? Was it efficient? She was determined to find out. If anyone complained she was sticking her nose where it didn't belong, they didn't dare say anything to her. She had always been good with sums and could read between the lines. Young as she was, she wasn't a ninny. She was her father's daughter and no one would make a fool of her.

She counted the wealth added to the family vaults,

ensured that food wasn't wasted and their deer weren't being hunted illegally.

She walked past the dairy, the laundry room, checking inventories and making sure everything was in good order. She knew everyone skimmed something off the top, but she wouldn't tolerate anything outrageous.

At the end of her review, she had fired one huntsman who had grown rich off bribes to allow people to hunt in her father's deer park and an accountant who was too lax with the tenants.

She was in the records room looking over the cost of firewood when a page opened the door.

She heard the swish of gowns and assumed it was one of her ladies come to fetch her for dinner or fresh air, so she was surprised when she looked up to see her father's mistress, Lady Bess, standing before her.

Mary set down her pen, making a note of where she left off.

"Good day," she said, trying to be as polite as possible.

"Lady Mary," she said, bobbing a deep respectful curtsy.

"Can I help you with something?" Something told her she would find this awkward. Despite the many months she had lived here, they had rarely spoken besides basic niceties and greeting each other at chapel.

"I think it is time you set aside your work here," she said rather stiffly.

"Why?"

"Well, for one thing I don't think your father would approve of you meddling in his accounts, and for another, I think you are beginning to look pale. He will blame me if you were to fall ill."

Mary was surprised. Of all things she was expecting Lady Bess to say, this was not one of them. The woman looked embarrassed but at the same time resolute.

"How would you know what my father would approve of? He had me taught. I don't need your permission to be here."

"Your father wrote to me…" Her voice trailed off.

"Wait, you are not telling me the full story. How would he know?" Mary was beginning to guess, but she wanted to hear it from Lady Bess herself.

"Your father was told—your father writes to me often and asks me for news."

"You are his spy." Mary's eyebrow arched. In a way she wasn't surprised. Her father must be keeping Lady Bess here for more than just his pleasure. She was useful to him in more ways than one. She wasn't the sort of woman you regarded as a threat.

"I look after his affairs here at Kenninghall," Lady Bess corrected her.

"I am doing the same." Mary looked down at the ledgers before her. She was not having this conversation. What she wished to do with her time was her business. Then what Lady Bess said sank in.

"What do you mean you look after his affairs?" Her voice was low as she spoke and she dared not look at her.

"He trusts me to oversee the running of Kenninghall."

Mary hummed. "Well, you should have kept these records in better order, then."

"They are rather well looked after. I am charitable when I can be. That huntsman might have let the common folk hunt your father's deer from time to time, but then that meat would feed their hungry families."

"I don't regret letting him go. He is lucky I did not have him arrested." Mary shrugged it off.

"Lady Mary, your father wishes for you to not concern yourself over such matters or go digging around in his records. No one else will be brave enough to tell you this, and I am only saying this because I have been asked. But I truly believe you should be enjoying yourself and preparing for court." Her voice trailed off.

Mary couldn't meet her gaze. She was struggling to keep a hold on her emotions. She wished for nothing more than to lash out at her and correct her. It wasn't true that her father would trust someone like her with such a task. She was a mistress, and once her father tired of her she would be out on the streets. How could he trust a whore more than his own flesh and blood?

"Leave me," Mary managed to say as steadily as she could.

"I-I am sorry. I don't want t-to upset His Grace." Lady Bess stuttered her way through an explanation.

Mary waved her away and waited for the tell-tale rustle of fabric to indicate Lady Bess had left the room before looking up. She glanced around. Other pages and clerks were going about their work pretending they hadn't heard anything. Mary felt like a child.

The thought that her father believed she was wasting her time and that her work here had no value was enough to make her want to fling her papers into the fire. She reminded herself to take deep breaths, but it didn't help the growing feeling of tightness in her chest.

Her father didn't see her as anything more than a silly child to be petted and cajoled into doing exactly as he wished. What more would she have to do to prove she could be useful?

She stayed until her candle had burned down to a mere stump before returning to her rooms. She didn't want the servants and men in her father's employ to gossip behind her back or see that she was retreating in defeat.

Mary's steps were heavy as she walked down the dark gallery, dimly lit by the last remnants of evening light.

"Lady Mary, we were just looking for you."

She jumped at being addressed. Her eyes focused on the figure of her uncle, who just appeared around the corner. A stranger following behind him.

"We startled you," he said, apologising with a hand to his heart to show his sincerity.

"You have, but it is not your fault," she said, forcing herself to keep her tone light. "I was lost in my own thoughts and you hadn't even been quiet." She looked at the man behind her uncle. He was blond and tall, with something foreign about him.

"May I introduce you to Master Hans Holbein," her uncle said, indicating to him.

Mary nodded politely in his direction. She was a duchess. She would not bow to him.

"You are a painter, I believe," she said.

"Was it the paint on my fingertips that gave me away?" He spoke at last, in a heavy accent. He was making a joke.

"No," she said, a genuine smile now. "Your reputation precedes you. I know the king invited you back. Your work is renowned. Why have you come to Kenninghall?"

He fixed his scrutinising gaze on her and she knew the answer. A hot flush spread across her cheeks and she coughed to clear her throat.

"He's here to paint your portrait," her uncle chimed in. "When you have time, let us know. He's here for a fortnight. Before heading to your husband to take his likeness."

"I appreciate how you say that as if I have a choice."

"Rest assured, my lady, that I don't have time to

force any unwilling person to sit still long enough for me to get a good image of them."

There was a slight haughtiness to his tone now. She wondered how he dared. But Mary supposed a painter with a reputation as good as his from a family as famous as his could afford to insult clients.

"I am not unwilling. Merely tired. We can speak tomorrow. I will sit for this portrait. Have no fear. I wouldn't pass up the opportunity to have you work on my likeness."

He bowed his head.

Her uncle looked at her as if he wanted to question her further, but now was not the time.

"Good evening, gentlemen," she said and continued on her way.

❧

"Turn your head to the right," he instructed her with all the severity of a schoolmaster. "Good. Now direct your gaze toward me without moving your head."

She obeyed.

"Now this is the hardest part," he said with a chuckle. "Don't move."

She opened her mouth to complain, but he spoke first.

"Ah no, what did I say? Don't move," he reminded her.

He moved behind the canvas. Soon Mary heard a

soft melody. Was it coming from him? She could crane her neck to see, but she dared not move. She didn't want to be forced to start again.

This was the third time he had attempted to sketch her. He claimed she was an elusive figure. In the early morning light he positioned her near a window so half her face was illuminated by the rays while the other half remained cloaked in shadow.

She was dressed in a pale blue gown, studded with white pearls. Around her waist she wore a jewelled belt of diamonds and sapphires. Every inch of her was sparkling in one way or another.

"Ah, one moment, I know what is missing," he said, as if a thought had struck him.

Mary heard him set down his tools and move about the room. This time she was too tempted not to look.

He was bent over the windowsill reaching out. A moment later he came up again. A large blooming rose in hand.

Hans Holbein clicked his tongue in disapproval.

"You moved and I told you not to," he said in a chiding tone, but his expression was one of contentment. Mary would bet he was more likely to smile than frown.

She squared her shoulders. Would he dare scold a duchess? "So I did," she said.

The challenge in her tone drew that smile from his lips as he placed the rose in her hand.

"Let's try again," he said before helping to reposition her just so.

His callused fingertips grazed her bare hand as he reached past her to rearrange the rosary on the table beside her.

"Pardon me, Your Grace," he muttered.

Mary prayed he couldn't see the goose bumps that had spread over her skin. She was incorrigible. She strived to ignore his presence and tried to focus on anything but him. In this moment her body was not her own, and she allowed him to position her to suit his purposes.

While he moved her hand to have it lie precariously on her stomach, a sign she might one day bear children, her eyes skirted across the room. First to Agnes, who was embroidering a cushion in silence nearby. Then to Hans's assistant leaning against the far wall, ready to come to his master's call.

Finally, to the rose that lay innocently in her other hand. Her grip on it was light, but she could feel its sharp thorns. A common white rose that grew in the hedgerows didn't belong in the portrait of a double duchess.

Mary was ready to say something, but she dared not question Hans Holbein as he continued arranging the table and the folds of her gown. She was sure he would paint the correct colours, perhaps enhance the rose to create the proper metaphor of a Tudor rose.

"It suits you better," he said, taking a step back to

get a better view of the tableau he'd created. "Softens you."

She focused her efforts on not moving, but she would be lying if she said his words didn't strike a chord in her. Mary wondered what he saw. She had a general idea of what he was to paint, the image of the perfect woman: fertile, obedient, and godly.

But Mary realised at that moment that she was hoping for more. She hoped that when he looked at her, he saw an attractive woman. That was a hard pill to swallow. She pushed down the impure thought. Not because she was afraid of her feelings, but because she was above him in both station and rank. Mary defiled herself even thinking of him, wishing he might think of her. She would push it out of her mind forever. She wouldn't even confess it to her priest.

Mary found her resolve tested by Hans Holbein's penetrating gaze. It unnerved her to have him looking at her like that, as if he could see into her very soul. She tried her best to hide her treacherous thoughts. She was a fool. This was his job. He was to look and study. He would be doing the same if it were her father sitting in this chair.

They sat in silence for two hours with only the sounds of his scribbling and scratching on the paper to fill the room.

When he finally released her, she found her legs were numb and her back sore.

She gave him a look of irritation, and though she

didn't voice any other complaints he still felt it necessary to chide her.

"Today was the toughest day. Tomorrow you shall return, but I shall instead focus on your gown, so you may tell your ladies to come play music for you to keep you occupied. It's not an easy task capturing a duchess like you on paper."

"Why do I get the sense you are laughing at me?" she said.

Hans gave her a grin, wiping his hands on a cloth, leaving a streak of black and grey.

"I meant no disrespect," he said. "I enjoy capturing my clients, but your features are so mercurial I found it hard to do so."

"I barely moved," she protested, her hands fidgeting with the edge of her sleeves.

"But your mind was travelling." He said this gently.

Mary glared, but her expression softened. This time he wasn't teasing her. "Then I am glad you were able to complete your sketch. I shall strive to be even stiller next time."

He bowed his head in thanks.

"May I see it?" Curiosity got the better of her.

"Not until it is finished, I'm afraid."

"But what if I do not like it?" She stopped herself from pouting like a child.

"I paint what I see. I don't flatter the sitter."

He was lucky he had such an easy manner that put her at ease rather than on the defensive.

"But I don't think you will be displeased with the final result," he added, looking back at the sketch hidden from her view. "No, it might be one of my best works to date, and I mean that as a compliment to you. Apologies if I was being too forward."

A fresh blush crept up her cheeks. She was glad he wasn't looking her way.

A servant came in carrying a fresh pewter of water, and another to stoke the fire.

"Then I shall leave you to your work. I will see you tomorrow after I break my fast," she said, standing to leave.

She watched him give her another one of his exaggerated bows. Her vanity was flattered by all the fuss he made of her.

Back in her rooms, the heavy gown and jewels were removed with care and tucked away in chests under lock and key. She kept a careful inventory of everything. The pearls alone were worth a tidy fortune.

"Do you think he will paint our likenesses next?" Joyce said, in an unnaturally high-pitched voice for her.

"If you can pay his fee," Mary said. Her tone was rather strained as the comb Joyce was running through her hair snagged on a knot. "I don't know if you could sit still long enough."

"Joyce thinks he's handsome. She would do

anything he asked." Agnes jumped in. Eager to tease her.

Mary looked from one lady to the next. A strange feeling overcame her, but she couldn't place it.

"I thought you were all busy making moon eyes at my uncle," she said, rather unkindly. "There are more important qualities to look for in a man than a pretty face."

A look passed between the two women.

"A skilled hand perhaps?" Agnes asked in all seriousness before the two burst into laughter.

Mary dismissed them with a frown. Being pent up indoors all day had clearly not done them any good. She hadn't realised what silly little chits they were. Was she any different? Again Mary pushed the thoughts to the back of her mind. She would be different.

She settled herself back at her writing desk, going over her letters and making a list of things she wanted to do over the next few days.

But she couldn't focus and in the end decided to play bowls.

※

The next day, Joyce and Agnes came to read to her as she sat for Holbein as he returned to studying her, but at least this time that gaze of his was focused in on her gown for the painting. As promised, there was an easier atmosphere today and plenty of jests.

However, this was obviously more distracting for the painter. As time ticked by Holbein looked ready to break and Mary, reading the room, sent her ladies away on errands. Joyce returned with her lute and played for them, leaving no room for conversation.

As the day ended, Holbein's gaze met hers.

"Thank you, Your Grace, for your intervention."

"I thought you might work better if you weren't busy fending them off." She paused, feeling she was being harsh. "They mean well, but truth be told they are probably bored here in the country. No amount of dance masters and other little entertainment will make up for the diminished society."

"That might be true, but all the same my wife would thank you for it," he said.

"Oh, you are married?" She was genuinely surprised, not that she had ever paid much attention to rumours circulating about a painter. Somehow she didn't imagine him as married. But painters weren't creatures from another world, and as she looked at him she determined he must be at least thirty. Certainly he was of an age that a man might have married at least once.

He nodded, and she was surprised by the pang of disappointment. "We were married for two years before I returned to England to earn my fortune. She is a good woman, my Elizabeth. We have two young children."

"She must be a patient woman to tolerate you living apart from her for so very long," she said, unsure why she was keeping the conversation going.

"Life is always full of surprises. She is a tolerant woman for putting up with me. We are happy together and apart. She does not need me to always be at her side. She is surrounded by my family and her own back in Germany." He was cleaning up his materials as he spoke. "We didn't marry for love, but I hope she doesn't come to hate me for my long absences."

Mary was embarrassed to have embarked on this conversation at all. Especially because she wasn't exactly innocent in her intentions.

"What made you become a painter?" She changed the topic.

"It is a family business. I am sure you know this already."

She looked away from his gaze.

"Lord Thomas tells me you love poetry," he said into the silence that prevailed.

"I do." Her response was curt, almost defensive.

"Why do you love it?"

"It's beautiful. The words strung together, flow like song. There's also the emotion they invoke." She trailed off at his smile.

"Then we are both lovers of art and beauty." He turned toward her. "You treasure words, while I seek to preserve the beauty I see in the world on canvas. My limitations are only my own talents. I hope to have many years to work on my craft."

"I predict you shall. Thank you for your time," Mary said, noting from the corner of her eyes that Joyce and Agnes had returned. "If you ever find yourself in need of new clients, know that you would have two eager ones here in my household."

He laughed. "It would be an honour, and perhaps another of you will be needed." He picked up the rose she had left on the table. "You mustn't forget this."

She took it without thinking. This felt like a declaration of something. Mary turned her mind back to business. "I must see the first one before committing to any further commissions."

"Clever of you, my lady." He bowed so low his blond head nearly touched the ground.

Mary thought he was being ridiculous, but the respect he showed her flattered her all the same. She swept out of the room, wondering when she would see him again.

Her last remaining weeks at Kenninghall were spent preparing for her return to court. She was happy to be as far from Lady Bess as possible.

CHAPTER 4

"It has been too long." Mary Shelton embraced her so tightly she thought she would be squeezed to death.

"It is good to see you as well." Mary pulled away, looking at her cousin. She was different.

Upon closer inspection it was hard to miss the new headdress and the ruby pendant pinned to her bodice. She had done very well for herself.

"What?" Mary Shelton said, pulling away, her hand smoothing over her gown. "Is something amiss?"

"No." Mary shook her head. "You look beautiful."

Her cousin beamed at her. "You don't look so bad yourself. I heard your father commissioned your portrait. Your husband is being painted as we speak."

"Yes, it was quite the experience," Mary said, but she knew her cousin was just trying to distract her.

The queen's presence chamber was crowded, so it

wasn't likely they could speak in private. This time Mary had been given a set of rooms all to herself.

"Come to my rooms tonight? We must speak in private," she said.

"Very well, but only if you promise to have good wine on hand," Mary Shelton said with a laugh. "Maybe we can make a party of it."

"No." Mary shook her head. "I don't want to be known around court as some pleasure-seeking woman."

"That is where you are mistaken. That's just the sort of woman that is popular at court right now." Mary Shelton shook her head as if she was disappointed. "I thought you'd be more forward thinking."

The queen laughed at something her companion said, pointing to her fool tumbling on the ground. The fool, renamed "Mary" after the former princess, was prone to outbursts and saying the most ridiculous things. Anne Boleyn had been eager to insult the Spanish at every turn; this was simply the most recent.

For her part, Mary Howard wished she had been given another name. England was filled with women named Mary. Sometimes it felt like they were all interchangeable. It certainly made it hard for her to know who someone was referring to when speaking of one Mary or another.

She looked in the direction of Mary Boleyn, the queen's sister, whose pale complexion and pretty round face had caught the eye of more than one king. Her daughter, Catherine Carey, was at court, not yet old enough to be given an official position but still richly decked and running around the Boleyn apartments. Even though she carried the name Carey, many whispered that she was the king's own daughter. There had never been a formal acknowledgment, but the king had certainly favoured Mary Boleyn by sending gifts for herself and the child.

Catherine also had a younger brother named Henry, who unfortunately had been born too late to benefit much from his status as the king's bastard son. Unlike Henry Fitzroy, he also carried the name of Carey and never received more than a purse of gold from the king. This wasn't surprising, as by the time he had been born the king's attention was already drifting away from one Boleyn sister to the other.

Mary had been young, and most of this knowledge she picked up as gossip from other ladies and servants. It certainly made for a good tale. There was nothing like a year at court to educate a girl about the harsh way of the world. Mary swore that she would never sell herself as cheaply as Mary Boleyn had.

Look what a bit of patience and cunning got Anne. A crown and a court fawning over her to get her attention. Even the king, despite their years together, was trying his best to please her. What was left for Mary Boleyn but to be forgotten by anyone who ever knew her?

"Margaret Douglas has finally been installed here as well," Mary Shelton pressed on. "She's left the service of Princess—I mean Lady Mary. Anyone with good sense has." She pointed a finger at a young woman passing by.

"Another Seymour sister has fled the Spanish queen's retinue for the court. You are lucky you came back when you did. Otherwise there might not be any room for you at all." Mary Shelton stopped with a laugh as a man suddenly jumped in their path.

Mary recognised Henry Norris. He moved with all the grace of a practiced dancer. He bowed, placing a kiss on her cousin's palm as he came up.

"Greetings, fairy, what brings you to this glen?" he said, his eyes twinkling with mischief.

Mary Shelton didn't pull away but put a hand over his as though she wished to pull him closer.

"I am here bringing the Duchess of Richmond and Somerset up to speed on all the news of the court."

"Ah," he said, his eyes raking over her. "Of course, foolish of me to not have noticed, but in your presence it is hard to notice anyone else. You outshine them all."

Mary was taken aback by such bawdy talk but tried to pretend like it didn't bother her since her cousin didn't flinch away.

Unfortunately for the three of them, the queen had noticed.

"What was that, Norris? Are you teasing those poor maids? Leave them alone."

"If the most glorious queen beckons me, then I

must come. For my heart is hers," he declared and was gone.

Mary blinked, trying to process this. Mary Shelton's gaze was following Norris through the crowd as he reached the queen, bowing.

Mary pulled her away to a more private alcove.

"Norris is courting you?" Her eyebrow was arched in a disapproving fashion.

Mary Shelton gave her a small smile. "He courts everyone. You saw how he is. But I do like him. You should see how well he rides in the lists. No one can unhorse him. He's fearless, and though he's not as tall or brawny as some of the other gentlemen, he's much stronger."

A little sigh escaped her lips, and Mary knew her cousin was lost in her thoughts.

"Court has—changed," she said with a sharp bluntness. Suddenly, she felt like a strict abbess, not a young duchess. "I'll get used to it. You don't understand what a different world Kenninghall is from this."

Mary Shelton nodded her head as if she understood. "It must have been very boring for you. Ah, look, there's Margaret," she said, waving the girl over.

Margaret Douglas was about their age, with glossy red hair that peeked out from beneath her French hood. It was this and her height that hinted at the royal blood that flowed through her veins.

Her mother had never been pretty. Not that Mary

had ever seen her in person but she heard gossip. Just before Margaret's birth the Scottish queen had travelled to England and been reunited with her family. Travel was the polite way of putting it. Queen Margaret had been forced to flee Scotland to give birth in some English convent. Her marriage to Archibald Douglas had been ill-advised, and she soon came to realise that, as she disposed of both her new husband and daughter not long after.

Mary examined Margaret's pleasing countenance more closely. She was lucky she didn't resemble her short, stocky mother. She looked more like Mary Tudor, the former queen of France, who had died last spring. She had been King Henry's favourite sister. The beautiful one that dazzled everyone. He would forgive her anything, even a clandestine marriage to Charles Brandon, Duke of Suffolk.

That was another story Mary had heard. But she wondered how much love there could have been if Charles had remarried so quickly after her death.

"Lady Margaret, you remember Lady Mary Fitzroy," Mary Shelton said with a curtsy.

"Of course." Her smile illuminated her face.

"It is wonderful to have you back at court," Mary said politely.

They stood in the alcove talking until Henry Norris and two other gentlemen came prancing over.

"You fairies shouldn't keep hiding away," he chided them.

"But it's amusing to see if you'd come looking." Mary Shelton didn't miss a beat.

Mary stood by Margaret, watching them toss compliments and jibes back and forth.

The other two gentlemen didn't dare approach them.

Mary thought she had Margaret's look of disapproval to thank for that. She liked her more and more with each passing moment.

The arrival of the king put all games to a stop as everyone diverged their full attention to him.

It was hard not to. He was a dominating presence, and his increasing girth only added to his majesty.

Mary watched as Anne flattered and flirted with him as if he was the only man in the room, despite the fact that a few moments ago she had been batting her lashes at the men of her court.

She turned to say something to Mary Shelton but found she had left the alcove.

"She's gone," Margaret whispered to her.

"Where?"

Margaret pointed and Mary finally found her cousin.

She had managed to bring herself to the front of the group, so when the king called for a dance and looked around for a partner it was Mary Shelton that his eyes settled on.

Mary's mouth was dry as she watched them take their positions in a pavane. Anne Boleyn was pretending not to notice. In the next dance, the king took another for his partner and Mary Shelton partnered with Henry Norris.

When had her cousin become so shameless?

Mary met Margaret's dark eyes. The question on the tip of her tongue, but she dared not ask her. They didn't know each other well enough for these sorts of conversations.

To her surprise, it was Margaret who took the first step.

"The queen is with child. Nothing has been confirmed, but we all suspect it. It's why she doesn't dance. She doesn't care who dances with the king or catches his fancy now."

"Why would you tell me?"

"It's common knowledge. I didn't want you to be worried," she said.

"Thank you, I appreciate it." Mary was still following the dancers as they spun round, flashes of silk and velvet. She had been left behind. Events were moving beyond her. A few months away and her cousin had grown and gained experience that made her feel as though she was still a child by comparison. She had even gained a paramour, from the looks Norris kept giving her.

Her view of the makeshift dance floor was blocked by a familiar figure.

"Uncle," she said with a bright smile. "How do you do?" She curtsied and he bowed to both of them.

"I am well," he said to her, but his eyes kept glancing toward Margaret.

"May I introduce you to Lady Margaret Douglas," Mary said with an amused smile.

Introductions over, he seemed eager to settle in for a long conversation but then stopped himself. "I have someone to introduce you to as well."

"One of your little friends?"

"Don't be rude, and I don't think he's that little," he teased and motioned a young man over. "This is Charles Blount."

Mary nodded to him in greeting. She had vague memories of his father, William Blount, Baron Mountjoy, the king's former tutor.

"He's an adept scholar. He's working on translating verses from Italian into English. I thought that might intrigue you," he said, giving her a knowing look.

Mary thought immediately of her book of poetry. He had succeeded in piquing her interest. She watched him as he bowed and parroted the expected niceties of court. He was just the sort of person you might overlook in a crowd, but he had a pleasing face and large kind eyes.

"Where did you learn Italian? Have you travelled that far?" she interrupted, unashamed.

A blush crept up his neck and made her smile.

"No, Lady. But I had the very best of tutors. My travels have taken me no farther than Cambridge and the court."

"I suppose we can forgive you for that. I haven't gone farther than Leeds, and it is likely I never will."

"Does your husband not live near York?" Even as he finished saying it he knew he had made a misstep.

"I haven't taken up residence with my husband." She tried to put it as politely as possible. Her uncle was amused and didn't hide it, which only made Charles more uncomfortable.

"I apologise. I don't know what I'm saying half the time."

The music came to a stop for the musicians to tune their instruments. New couples were stepping onto the dance floor.

Almost on a whim, Lady Margaret mentioned her desire to dance, and her uncle, playing the part of the chivalrous knight, indulged her fancy.

"Would you like to dance as well?" Charles Blount said in a whisper.

Deciding that being on the side-lines alone was undesirable, she nodded and let him lead her out.

The dance was another pavane, nothing fast or complicated. Her face was impassive as they were brought together and separated again as the steps dictated.

The music faded and they went their separate ways.

She wondered if his work with paper and pen was more impressive than his footwork.

Mary was in her apartments, watching Agnes and Joyce put away her jewels. She had been informed by her father's man that her portrait was ready. An appointment was scheduled for the following day with the painter. She had been dying to see it.

A part of her was also eager to see Hans and make some amends for acting like a fool. She remembered everything from those few days and felt nothing but embarrassment as she thought of them. Had she been attempting to flirt with him? Did he think she was? Each thought was equally horrifying. If she were going to fall in love and have a string of affairs, then it would not be with some lowly painter.

She remembered Blount and how ill at ease he had been in her presence, to the point he was always saying the wrong thing. Was that how she had appeared to Holbein? She couldn't bear to think someone thought so poorly of her. You would think she hadn't been raised and educated by one of the richest families in England.

Her father's rooms were close to her own. They were larger and better kept, of course. Mary would never have precedence over him until her husband truly came into his own. For now they were both still pretending to be great lords and ladies of the land. It was an honour that she had even been allocated rooms. She doubted if the court moved away from Hampton

Court that she would continue to be allotted such favour.

"Good day, Father," she said with a deep curtsy.

"You look well." He glanced her way. "Been keeping busy in the queen's rooms?"

She nodded.

"Good, it's never good to be idle," he said with a half-smile.

Mary felt the urge to ask him point blank about why he had sent her to Kenninghall under false pretences, but she couldn't bring herself to ruin his good mood.

Then, without any fanfare, Hans Holbein came in, followed by the covered portrait carried in by two youths.

He bowed to her father first before paying his respects to her. She greeted him nonchalantly, wondering if perhaps there was any chance he had guessed her thoughts all those weeks ago when she had been disappointed to discover he was married.

"My lord, this is some of my best work," the young painter promised, but her father was unimpressed.

"Let's see what my gold has bought," her father said.

Mary watched with bated breath as Holbein lifted off the heavy coverings of the portrait. In that second before it was revealed she was scared all over again. This painting of her would live on forever. What if he had made her look ugly? She had seen herself in a mirror before. She knew she was not hideous, but that didn't mean her portrait would not be.

Then there it was. She bit back a gasp to see herself so lifelike painted on the canvas. Something about the way he had captured her eyes. It was as if she was about to entrap someone in a net. She stepped closer to it, wondering what would happen if she touched it. Would she be transported back into that room in Kenninghall, the rose in her hand?

Her father grunted.

She couldn't tell if it was disapproval or not.

"This looks rather fantastical," he said at last, looking from her to Holbein. "I pictured you painting her differently. You know the ones with the face staring straight at you."

"You hadn't specified exactly what or how you wanted me to paint her," Holbein said defensively. "We discussed symbolism and important motifs, nothing more."

They argued for some time over the schematics.

Mary took in the whole painting with a more critical eye. She could see what her father meant. This could be some painting of a Madonna or something out of antiquity. He had given her skin a glow.

But hearing him argue about the technique and the symbolism made Mary aware that this was nothing to him. Everything had been contrived in some way by her father.

Holbein had merely been doing his job, and in this

case he had let his creativity run wild. She was a little fool to imagine Holbein had been contriving some way of giving her a flower. Who knew it would take so little to trick a Howard? Her heart, which had been hammering in her chest, slowed. She felt at peace. How easy it was to come back to earth.

She thought she was above taking an interest in men and wishing herself in love. It was humbling to know she was just like every other being: pining for love, reading too much into things. Mary consoled her injured pride with the fact that at least she had recovered easily.

"Mary." Her father's voice jolted her out of her reverie.

She saw both men looking at her. Somewhere she recalled hearing her father ask her what she thought of the painting.

She cleared her throat, sensing a trap. "It's beautifully done, but I cannot vouch for the overall—painting. It would be vain of me to call it beautiful or ugly. You must be an impartial judge and guide me in this."

His eyebrow arched at her reply, but he turned back to Holbein. "Yes, I suppose I cannot argue about the quality of it. You have a deft touch. I don't like seeing my daughter painted as—this would invite people to look too much."

"If they do it is because she is becoming a great lady of this land," Holbein said. "Her appearance," he added with a shrug. "That she cannot help, my lord. My paintbrush doesn't lie."

Her father cleared his throat. "Very well. As I said, my criticism never lay with the quality."

Mary watched the two men debate over the fate of this painting. Holbein defending his work, her father unsure if he should be patronising a man who made his daughter look like a goddess out of a fairy story.

"You must paint another, quarter portrait," she said in between their squabbling. "One like the one you did of the queen. If you have the time in your schedule."

Holbein's gaze turned to her. She thought she saw laughter in his eyes.

"That is an excellent suggestion, Your Grace." He looked at her father with a tilt of his head. "I can begin next week. With your approval, of course."

Her father merely nodded. "Have this sent to Kenninghall. It shall hang in the gallery there."

The two servants covered and carted off the painting. Mary almost wished she had asked to keep it in her rooms. It seemed to her a waste to have it tucked away in the country.

"You shall make matching portraits of my daughter and her husband, the duke. They can hang here in my presence chamber," he stipulated.

Holbein clapped his hands together as if to seal their contract. "Excellent."

Mary watched him leave, glad to have made him so happy.

"Artists are all thieves," her father muttered under his breath.

"What's a few gold pieces?" Mary said. "The king himself wants Holbein to paint him."

"I haven't heard him say that," he said.

"Oh, he mentioned it in passing while visiting the queen. I think he plans on having a whole family portrait commissioned. He liked the one Thomas More ordered."

Her father hummed. Then his eyes narrowed. "You'd best not mention More at court. The king is displeased with him at present."

"Oh?"

Her father didn't explain further but said, "He'll come around, of course. How could you not obey your prince?"

That was the way with her father. No one should fight or go against the law of God and nature. A subject obeys his king. A child obeys their father.

That night, she sat with a candle at her writing desk. She had been unable to sleep and for the first time gave in to the strong urge to put ink to paper.

Her emotions were so overwhelming that this was surely the only way to make sense of them.

She began to write.

Can you see
I am weak?
I will bend, for that is my way,

Behold my hands—naked,
Without defence I ask what now?

She finished the poem, adding a few more stanzas, changing a few words here and there. She thought of a title and scrawled the word "Confessions" on top.

⁂

Mary Shelton continued on playing her games, flirting with every man in sight, accepting gifts and bribes. She was one of the most popular and talked about ladies of the court. If only she hadn't won this favour by being so loose with her favours. Under any other circumstances, perhaps she could have been another Anne Boleyn and risen to untold greatness.

Mary didn't blame her cousin. She knew how the family had pushed her down this path. It wasn't her fault. Besides, she had a new understanding of what was driving her forward. It felt nice to feel loved and noticed. Being admired was intoxicating. You could never get enough.

So Mary let her cousin drift further away from her and focused on being grateful to have Margaret Douglas as a companion. They had a lot in common, and conversation between them was easy. Margaret loved writing poetry as much as Mary enjoyed reading it.

So it was to Margaret that Mary showed her first poem.

Mary was too embarrassed to watch Margaret reading her work, so she focused her attention on the storm outside. It was an early winter storm, and the weather wasn't cold enough. She was sure the snow would melt by tomorrow, but the howling wind outside made her shiver nonetheless. It whipped the snow around in a vortex of white, making it hard to see.

"It's well done," Margaret said. "You shouldn't be so hesitant about your work. I remember you claimed you couldn't write, but here is proof you can."

Mary was uneasy. "Thank you for saying that. I never—I suppose I was scared to try." She shrugged. "I know how critical I can be of others. I didn't wish to invite the criticism upon myself."

Margaret was sympathetic but wouldn't relent. "Don't become hypocritical. But don't force yourself either."

Mary acknowledged her point.

"So what now?"

A twinkle of mischief in Margaret's eyes made Mary regret ever agreeing with her.

"There are some people you might be interested in meeting."

Having secret meetings at court was a misnomer. There was no privacy here. Servants could be bribed to look the other way, guards paid to keep people out, but word inevitably got out. Everyone knew everyone's business. They also knew or could make assumptions about what was happening behind closed doors. Those assumptions were usually more dangerous than the truth.

Mary and Margaret contrived a different plan: to meet in plain sight.

The queen's rooms were never quiet or empty for long. Men and women came and went. She could no longer ride out nor go hawking, so besides walking in the gardens and picnics they were always in the palace. Now that the weather had taken a turn for the worse, even the king remained indoors.

Margaret and her friends, a gaggle of other poetry aficionados, met in the queen's rooms to discuss poetry, share what they wrote, and pass it among each other. They welcomed Mary into the fold. Most had known of her work already. Mary thrived in this new group. It was exciting to be taking part in something for a change.

The king and queen were sitting side by side at dinner, their heads pressed together in deep conversation.

Mary ate at the table with all the other ladies. Her husband had not yet arrived, and she doubted they would be forced to sit together even if he had.

Someone tapped her shoulder. Her uncle was there, in a new green and tan suit.

"Court life suits you," she said.

He smiled. "The same could be said about you."

Mary caught how his eyes kept darting among the other ladies.

"If you've come here just so I can make introductions to all the eligible ladies, then you are barking up the wrong tree," she sniffed, pretending to have been insulted.

He placed a hand over his heart in mock hurt.

"No, never," he said. Then he leaned closer. "Those friends of mine that you were so curious about. They are interested to meet you. Are you intent on continuing your study of poetry?"

She was suddenly very aware of her heart pounding wildly in her chest. "Yes, I would."

"Something told me you would be," he said, then patted her shoulder. "I will see you later."

The holiday season would be upon them soon, and there was a sense of anticipation in the air as everyone waited for the queen to announce her condition.

She turned to her dinner partner only to see Margaret's gaze following her uncle as he moved around the dining hall toward his seat.

"You like him?" Mary said in mild surprise at the realisation.

"Like who?"

Mary nudged her under the table. "You know who

I mean." She grinned. "Not that I understand why, but the two of you seem keen on continuing to make eyes at each other when you think the other isn't looking."

Margaret remained tight-lipped and Mary didn't press her any further. Objectively, she knew it wasn't surprising at all that two handsome people would be drawn to each other.

It might even be a good match for her uncle, who would marry into the royal family and to a woman with a large dowry. However, would the king support such a match?

She didn't see why not.

Everyone was too busy watching the queen these days to be watching the ladies of her bedchamber. Everyone wondered when the queen might make some formal announcement of her condition.

Bets were being placed left and right. The prying eyes of laundresses and maids monitored her plate and bedsheets.

Mary, who often assisted the queen to get dressed, could see no sign of a child herself. When Anne had been pregnant with Elizabeth, she had been sick in the mornings and, despite eating little, her stomach had grown. This time the opposite was true. Despite the queen's hearty appetite, she was shrinking into herself. Her gowns falling loose about her person so they had to tie her bodices tighter and tighter. Mary could not claim to be an expert in such matters, but if she were asked to place a bet she wouldn't put any money on a spring or summer child.

She was sitting with Margaret, Mary Shelton, and two other ladies of their circle when the king entered the room. His eyes went straight to Anne and he paid her the normal compliments of a husband to his most beloved wife.

They settled in to play cards. Mary Shelton's eyes held a sort of hunger as she regarded them. Everyone noted she hadn't been invited to play.

Music was played and the room settled in to conversation. Outside another storm was raging. There would be nothing else to do until later in the evening when the king might play tennis.

From the corner of her eye Mary caught the familiar figure of her uncle approaching, two men flanking him on either side. She recognised Sir Francis Bryan but not the other gentleman.

She turned to greet him with a smile and invite them all to sit.

Introductions were made, and she learned the gentleman was none other than Thomas Wyatt.

"I know that name," she said with a frown, trying to recall where she had heard it before.

"Perhaps you know of my father, Sir Henry Wyatt. He was the king's lord treasurer for a time, among a much greater career. He's now retired to the country," the man said.

She nodded, but she didn't think that was the case. There was more to him than simply being one of many courtiers at court. Mary Shelton was busy trying to catch his attention, so it might have been from this quarter that she had heard the name of Thomas Wyatt.

He was striking with his thick dark hair and equally dark eyes. Even his clothing stood out. Among the brightly dressed courtiers he had picked a black suit with fine silver embroidery on his jacket and slashed sleeves that exposed the crisp white linen shirt beneath. She caught the look of amusement as he caught her looking. Mary knew then that he was a man who was very much aware of his charms and how to use them to the best advantage.

Beside him Sir Francis Bryan had chosen a more flamboyant style. Bright hues of orange and gold tissue with a chain of white opals hung around his neck.

Perhaps he dressed in such outrageous colours on purpose, knowing that no matter what he wore, your gaze was drawn to his eye. The one that was no longer there. The eye patch he wore today was of soft black velvet, but Mary recalled seeing him wearing more elaborate styles, some decorated with jewels. On the day of Anne's coronation he wore one embroidered with her emblem: the white falcon.

They spoke of ordinary things, but slowly something in their conversation shifted. Their words took on a lyrical turn of phrase. They replied to each other with rhymes.

It no longer felt like a conversation about the harvest or a journey by ship to Calais. It was a contest of verse.

Mary, leaning forward on her stool, was caught by surprise when Wyatt directed a sharp phrase toward her. She flushed with embarrassment as she caught the meaning, but she didn't run scared.

"Is it not better for one to know their place than to go bumbling through their paces?" She spun it back around.

She was rewarded by his laugh. "I concede the point, to the most attentive of ladies. May she one day be my teacher."

The group broke off from their little game.

"Wyatt, leave her alone."

Mary thought she could hear a threat behind her uncle's drawling voice.

Wyatt shrugged, picking at some invisible lint on his sleeve.

"That's just how he is," Margaret said. "He's been sour ever since returning from Italy."

Mary wanted to ask how she had known Wyatt and why she'd never brought him up before. But the mention of Italy caught her interest more.

"You've gone that far?" she asked him.

"I've travelled to the moon and back," he

responded, rather sardonically. "But yes, I've gone to most places you can think of."

"Russia?" she asked.

Silence. Then a heavy sigh. "No, not Russia. But I've been as far as Constantinople."

"If you have," Francis Bryan said with a wide grin, "then I have two eyes."

Wyatt frowned at him and his eye patch. "I was merely trying to impress the lady," he said, with a half-hearted wink in her direction.

"You change your tack so quickly, it is hard to keep up," Mary said, not knowing what to think. Hadn't he been insulting her moments ago?

Mary Shelton laughed, placing a hand on her arm for reassurance. "Be flattered Master Wyatt pays any attention to you at all."

"If that was an invitation, Lady Mary, just let me know." He was giving her his full attention now.

Mary Shelton leaned forward, under the pretence of rearranging her skirts, giving him a good look at her cleavage. As she straightened up she shook her head. "Not this time, I'm afraid."

"Aiming higher?" Again the teasing.

"Definitely higher than yourself." A look of scorn on her face.

Mary watched the exchange with growing amusement. She was catching on to how Wyatt operated.

Sir Francis Bryan, ever observant, noticed that the

king and queen had finished their game and nudged Thomas. Their brief foray had to end.

"Until next time, Lady Mary," Wyatt said to Mary Shelton. His gaze swept over them, and with a tilt of his head he was gone.

Mary stared after them.

"Well, that was interesting," she said, looking first to Margaret and then Mary Shelton.

"Welcome back to court," Mary Shelton said with a grin.

CHAPTER 5

The king and queen wanted this—their first Christmas together as man and wife—to be the grandest in recorded history. This meant that coin poured out from the king's treasury. They spent lavishly on banquets, musicians, pageants, and gifts for each other.

The queen danced and laughed—the happiest of women. Every night she captured the attention of the court and the hearts of all who beheld her.

Underneath this exuberance and energy was an anxiety that no one dared name. On the eve of Christmas Day, the queen's sheets had been stained red with her menstrual blood. She was not carrying a prince in her womb. All this speculation and betting for weeks had been for nothing.

The maids and laundresses were blamed for telling lies and losing track of her cycle. No one looked at Anne, not yet. After all, nothing had been announced.

But Mary suspected the queen had been hopeful. Each night she was one of the chosen few given the privilege to help her undress and get ready for bed. They would peel away her majesty layer by layer, until she was left in a linen shift. She was transformed from a queen to a thin pale woman, and her hand would drift unthinking to her stomach. A sadness would creep into her eyes, but then Anne would blink and move her hand away. Her expression transformed into one of resolute confidence.

Mary knew, they all knew, that Anne Boleyn had promised the king a son. What would happen if she could not give him one?

With time the queen's disappointment turned to wrath. That was when her enemies began to cast furtive glances around to see who might defend them.

But there could be no safe haven for them, not while Anne had the king twisted around her finger, obedient to her every demand. It wasn't like before when they were still courting and he would bend over backward to please her. But he had learned he could mould England and its people to be what he wanted. So more often than not her insistence wore down his hesitancy.

The words in the books she had shown him had wooed him. The debates and Latin texts that said no one was above a king, except for God. A few years ago,

Thomas More had burned heretical texts such as these in a great pyre, alongside the men who read and distributed them.

No wonder many called Anne Boleyn the heretic queen.

Now they suited King Henry's vanity. He wouldn't allow the Bible to be translated into English for the common people to read, but he wanted to be the first among men, obedient to no one else but God.

Mary didn't trouble herself too much about this. Unlike her father, whose religion was deep rooted, she was flexible in her devotion. She didn't question the king's divine right. It made sense to her that the king should be head of the church.

Besides, he was here, commanding and leading England as he saw fit. The pope was some faraway figure who threatened the realm with war, but he hadn't been able to bring down the anger of God on England as he swore he would do. He was too scared to even excommunicate Henry Tudor. Mary wasn't frightened of him, but she was frightened of the king, whose rages were becoming more frequent these days as he fought to bend the nobles and notable figures of England to his will.

Mary was glad no one troubled themselves to ask what she or any other woman thought about it. She focused instead of the pleasantries of poetry, hunting, and dancing.

She didn't envy the men in parliament debating

this great matter. Nor did she envy the queen, who was making herself sick arguing with her scholars about how to put forth a better case.

At last they drew up a document called the Act of Succession. Every man and woman in the kingdom had to sign. It declared that Henry was head of the church, that he could pick his successors. The most notable absence was that of his daughter, Mary. He called his own child a bastard and would make her sign an oath acknowledging this.

Mary thought this was cruel of him. It didn't matter how many presents he showered on her cousin or his current queen. She couldn't forget how his face had gone red with rage when they told him his daughter declared she would never sign the act. He had sent the Duke of Norfolk to threaten her with death if she didn't change her mind.

When the Act of Succession was put before Mary Tudor again, she still refused to sign. Henry Tudor placed her under house arrest. The king couldn't have her brought to the tower and executed without causing an international crisis. As long as Katherine of Aragon lived she was safe. Mary Howard doubted he would extend the same favour to her if she refused.

The Act of Succession appalled many. At first some couldn't bring themselves to swear against their conscience, but at the end of the day fear of the axe was greater than fear of retribution in the afterlife. Mary knew that those devout souls would argue they had been coerced. They would sleep easier at night thinking both their God and king were pleased.

In the end, of the people who mattered, only two men remained obstinate. They stood firm against the king and his desires. They argued—publicly—that he was wrong, that he was leading England down the path to damnation.

Mary knew with certainty that they would be cut down. It was only a matter of when.

By the spring of 1534, Thomas More and Bishop Fisher were in the Tower of London. Everyone expected them to bow to the king's desire.

She had been in the room when her father assured the lord chancellor that some time in those cold cells would make More and Fisher see sense. It wouldn't be long before they apologised and signed the act. By Christmas they would be forgiven and back in the king's favour.

Her father had sounded sincere as he spoke. But Mary wondered if her father was lying to himself as well as the lord chancellor. Even if they swore that they had been wrong, she didn't think the king would just forget.

While the world around her was shifting with the changing tide, Mary found her escape in the small circle of like-minded people she and her uncle had gathered. They met to discuss and share poetry. Plans were made to one day publish the works they had gathered.

For all his flirtatiousness and his haughtiness, Thomas Wyatt was a skilled poet and performer. When he read his poems out loud or played songs he had composed on the lute, no one could look away.

Mary struggled with her jealousy and awe of him. She wished she had a drop of his skill. They were in the gardens, and the queen nearby made a bet on who was the better musician, Mark Smeaton or Thomas Wyatt. Mary watched money exchanging hands. Everyone was betting on Wyatt.

"He's had years of practice on you," someone said behind her.

She whipped around, startled to find Sir Francis Bryan standing close. He glinted in the sun. She wasn't sure how he had managed to sneak up behind her in that ridiculous turquoise suit. He had that knowing look in his eye, as if he had read her thoughts.

"I know I will never match him in skill," she said, reprimanding him with a pointed stare for scaring her. "But it doesn't stop me from hoping to discover my hidden talent."

Mary watched his gaze travel back to Thomas, listening to him improvise some verse.

"I think with some practice you will outshine him. You are much better to look at," he said lazily.

Mary bit back a laugh. She had become immune to his shocking choice of words. "No, sir. I cannot dedicate myself to the craft like he can. So I will have to concede he won a war we never fought."

"We need more men like you in the war room," Francis said with a toothy grin. He placed his hands on his hips, appraising her. She didn't flinch.

"I'd be happy to advise you," she said, then frowned. "Are we going to war?"

The smile in his eyes died to be replaced by steel. "I am to leave England for a while. Will you do me a favour? Watch that uncle of yours." He avoided the question altogether.

"Which one?" she teased, but she was in no doubt of which uncle he was referring to. "I will try," Mary amended. "But why?"

"Because I ask it of you."

She frowned and tried again. "What do I have to watch out for?"

His grip on her arm was light as he pulled her farther from the crowd but not completely out of sight. "He's halfway in love with your friend Lady Margaret. That would be a dangerous road for them to tread on. Watch him. Watch her."

Mary gaped at him. "You can't be serious." But there was nothing in his appearance or countenance to indicate otherwise. "I'll do my best."

"They can do nothing unless the king approves. Maybe your father can snag another Tudor for the Howards through marriage, but..."

She stopped him from saying the words. "I know. And the king isn't in a forgiving mood. Where are you going?"

The mischievous gleam in his eye was back. "To Utopia."

"Ha."

Mary appreciated the clever answer. It would have been characteristic of him to spew out nonsense, but Utopia meant Thomas More, and he meant the pope and old faith. Maybe she was mistaken, but she would put her money on him being in Rome very soon. She shivered. It was an open secret that he wielded a dagger in the dark on the king's behalf, striking down enemies before they struck. Mary almost wanted to ask who he was going after this time.

He craned his neck around. "You'd best get back. I think you are needed."

Mary knew better than to argue with him. She materialised by the queen's side, excusing her absence.

Over the next few days she paid close attention to Margaret Douglas and her uncle. At first she didn't see anything that would be a cause for concern. Maybe Sir Francis Bryan was just being overly cautious.

Mary continued her vigil but still nothing. They never spoke to one another, never even looked at one another if they could help it. Then it struck her how odd that was.

Suddenly, it seemed as though they were working a

bit too hard to make sure they didn't interact with one another.

She pulled her cousin aside and questioned her with all the harshness of a lawyer trying to uncover the truth.

"Do you know something?" she asked, her tone as firm as the grip on Mary Shelton's arm.

At first she smiled coyly and avoided answering.

"How could I know? Aren't the two of you great friends? Ask her yourself."

"They wouldn't tell me, but you might have seen something I have not. This is very important." Mary pushed her cousin. She was thinking of those secret late-night parties her cousin snuck off to. Maybe she had seen or heard something.

Finally, she saw Mary Shelton hesitate and think harder.

"Henry Norris mentioned your uncle has been miserable and spends most of his time writing poetry rather than attending to his duties."

"And Margaret?" Mary pushed.

A gleam appeared in Mary Shelton's eye. "You think he's pining after her. How romantic."

Mary shook her head. "You mean how dangerous."

"You can't help who you love. It's only a harmless flirtation," Mary Shelton said, disagreeing with her.

Mary knew it would be futile to argue with her. The very next day she contrived to meet her uncle in the gardens. The first signs of spring were all around, and the sun overhead was warm.

Agnes and Joyce walked a few steps behind her. She couldn't just go sneaking around the palace alone without drawing suspicion. The last thing Mary wanted was rumours floating about that she was involved in some clandestine affair. She looked back at them, deciding she would have to trust them not to report anything they overheard. Perhaps it was foolish of her, but she had no choice.

Her uncle materialised, bowing to them and winking at her ladies, which left the two girls blushing red.

"You wished to speak to me?"

Mary suspected he was laughing at her, and he continued to tease her for her serious expression. At last the question came spilling out, and not at all in the suave way she had planned to ask.

"What have you heard?" he asked.

"Nothing to concern yourself about," she said, then shrugged. "People have been noticing your strange behaviour. Namely Sir Francis Bryan and now myself. Even Henry Norris says you are sick with love for someone."

Her uncle had gone a shade or two paler. "Bryan suspects?" He took off his cap, running his hand through his hair. A nervous gesture.

"Don't worry," she began and almost said that he would not betray his friend, but how could she be sure?

"He doesn't think it's serious. At least not yet. So tell me, is it serious?"

Her uncle shook his head, but even as he spoke Mary could hear the lie. "It's just a bit of fun. Courtly love and poetry. We've done nothing besides write a few verses to each other. The queen gets hundreds of presents and poems written about her and no one bats an eye. This is innocent."

"So you swear nothing is going on?" she whispered. "Nothing that would land either of you in trouble?"

"Our very existence is an invitation for trouble. But no, this is innocent." He turned away from her and she couldn't make out his expression. "It's playacting. We are both bored and looking for some excitement."

"I'm not going to pretend I'm some experienced courtier, but even I can see the danger of it," she said.

Mary thought she heard a sound behind them and turned to see her older brother and her husband coming around the bend of the path. She coughed to alert her uncle and put on a bright courteous smile as they stopped and waited for the two men to catch up to them.

"I was told we might find you here, sister," her brother said, looking from one to another with a wide grin on his face. "A chilly day to be walking outside. Shouldn't you be serving the queen?"

"She's reading with her other ladies," Mary said defensively. Her gaze drifted to her husband, standing there with an imperious look on his face. If he was looking for something to criticise, he wouldn't find it.

"Well, the fresh air has certainly put some colour in your cheeks for once." He shared a smile with Fitzroy at the backhanded compliment.

Mary tried not to let any emotion show on her face. He was such a child to have been making sport of her like this. As if she cared what she looked like. Of course, like any person, she hoped she was attractive, but she also knew she didn't have to be. Her birth and lineage made sure she would always be a person of consequence. Besides, she wasn't some faerie creature that never aged. Sooner or later she would lose her looks. She wanted to say all of this to them, but she held back, not wishing to give them more ammunition.

"What were the two of you talking about so animatedly?" her husband asked.

"The weather," she snapped, then knew she had made a mistake. She saw how his eyes narrowed and clouded over with suspicion or anger. She took on a more subservient demeanour. "Apologies, my brother knows how to get under my skin. We were deciding who to bet on in the next tournament. Is that what brings you to London this time of year?"

"Yes, your brother is going to run in the lists," Fitzroy said flippantly. He had grown bored of her. Now his eyes rested on her ladies-in-waiting. She had the impression he didn't have the best of intentions as he regarded them.

One of her brother's favourite pastimes was whoring, and she wondered if he had dragged her husband along. She would hate if he spent their money on loose women. Perhaps, like the king, her husband had an exaggerated sense of his handsomeness and would find it insulting to visit brothels. He certainly looked at her ladies as if he expected them to fall all over themselves with excitement at him noticing them.

"I'm surprised father will let you," she said without thinking. Her brother was an earl, not a child that could be commanded. He had more freedom than she did, even though he was still beholden to their father and owed him obedience.

"Let's go inside," her uncle broke in before this conversation could turn into a brawl.

It was a strange situation to be in. The three men stared at each other, unsure of how to proceed. Her uncle had seniority, but Fitzroy held the higher rank, followed by her brother. However, they respected Thomas Howard the younger enough to listen to him, and Mary was spared.

The appearance of her husband changed little for her. Their apartments were separate from each other in the fear they might be tempted to consummate the marriage. It wouldn't matter if Mary protested she wanted nothing to do with him.

This way was easier and no one's feelings got hurt. Of course, there was always the possibility that Fitzroy would convince the king and her father to give him permission to make the marriage true. She prayed neither of them would give in to his demands. As long as Fitzroy continued acting like a spoiled child, wanting something because he had been told no, she would be safe.

Wanting to be in her bed had nothing to do with love or lust. He wanted to be regarded as a man. She was sure he had talked himself into believing that fathering a child on her was one way to prove it. Mary knew her duty, but she preferred things the way they were. Nothing about him appealed to her. She was sure he felt the same. After all, he dreamed of glory, she was hardly the princess he was expecting to marry. Maybe he would wish to set the marriage aside. Or if Anne had a son, then Fitzroy wouldn't be such an important asset and her father would find a way to annul the marriage. Mary enjoyed being a duchess, but if things couldn't remain as they were then she'd rather be rid of him despite the embarrassment.

Why was nothing simple?

"You are so lucky," Margaret said as they sat atop their horses, watching their falcons in flight.

"I am?" Mary glanced toward her. There was a sad look on Margaret's face.

"I wish to be in love and married," Margaret

confessed to her. "I fear I shall never be allowed to leave the king's court."

"I am married but neither loved or in love," Mary pointed out. Then, realising what she had said, she glanced around to see if anyone had overheard. Luckily, the rest of the court was huddled around Anne Boleyn, praising her skill as her hawk returned with her prey.

"I suppose. But you never know," Margaret said. "It is still better than being trapped as a maid forever. I might as well be a nun. Then at least I would have a vocation."

"I don't think nuns are allowed to write verse," Mary said with a chuckle.

Margaret looked back at her, then laughed. "You are right. As always. Sometimes I forget you are the younger. I should be the one giving you advice."

Mary understood her frustration. The French ambassador had suggested a match for Margaret, but the king had rejected it without even considering it. Margaret was an heir to the English throne, and there weren't very many Tudor heirs at the moment. Mary stared at the queen's lithe form. There was no sign yet of that changing.

The queen had recently banished her sister from court. She had returned from the summer progress with a big belly and a secret marriage. Anne Boleyn could have forgiven her sister anything else but this. It was an insult to her to see her sister so plump, pretty, and fertile, a direct contrast to herself. So Mary Boleyn and her children and new husband were all sent away in shame and disgrace. No one would lift a finger to help them.

Rumour was that they were living like peasants in the country somewhere. Mary felt bad for them, but there was nothing she could do even if she wanted to. Anne Boleyn ruled all.

Mary held out her gloved hand, calling out to her falcon. Obedient, it glided back, landing softly on her hand. She rewarded it with a piece of meat before handing the bird to her falconer to be hooded again. She was growing tired and wanted to rest.

"I'll come back with you," Margaret said.

"Are you sure?" Mary teased. "Why not stay and see if you can catch yourself a husband here?"

"No one here is worth having," she replied, a wistful expression on her face.

Mary was reminded of Sir Francis Bryan's warning. She looked around at the men that rode out with them. There were very few notable persons that weren't here, but her uncle was among them. She swallowed hard and pushed the thought from her mind. Margaret was just talking. She didn't mean anything by it.

They were watching the king play tennis. His opponent, Francis Weston, struggled to return his volleys. Mary watched with more interest than usual. She and Margaret had placed heavy bets on this game.

Boredom had crept over the court, and many had turned to such vices. There was nothing like a bit of risk to make your heart skip a beat.

Back and forth the ball went, the men running around the court. At first they had been evenly matched, but the king outpaced Weston in endurance, despite being nearly twice his age.

In the end, the king won. Mary hid her disappointment. That was ten pounds gone just like that. The watching crowd applauded the victor, while behind the scenes, money was being collected and distributed.

A tap on Mary's elbow made her turn around. There was the blue-eyed gallant from before, a half-hidden smile on his lips and an open purse outstretched to her.

"I believe that was ten pounds," he said in a soft tone.

Mary reached into her own purse for it. "I thought my bet was with Sir William Brereton." She pouted, hesitating to hand it over.

"I am acting as his page today, collecting his debts," he replied smoothly.

Mary frowned in reply. "Doesn't that injure your pride?"

"No. Not when I can find an excuse to speak to

such lovely ladies," he said with an exaggerated bow. She was reminded of Hans Holbein and smiled. Margaret, who had been at her side, turned to see who had been talking to her friend.

"You flatterer," she said to his down-turned blond head. "How much do I owe?"

"I believe it was five pounds," Charles Blount said after consulting a list.

Margaret groaned but handed it over without complaint.

"You'd think you'd forgive us our debts," Mary said, teasing. "Since we are such lovely ladies." But she too handed over the coin.

He laughed. "But how would you ever learn to stop gambling?"

Both Mary and Margaret rolled their eyes.

"Have you never gambled?" Mary asked.

"Once, and then I learned it wasn't for me," he said.

Mary wanted to ask more, but Margaret spoke before she could.

"You don't understand the thrill of it," Margaret said, waving him away. "Now begone, back to your master."

He obeyed.

Mary watched him make his way through the crowd, stopping every now and then to speak to someone. He seemed like he was drifting through this world, unbothered by the corruption and vice around him.

"I'll bet you a shilling he is an avid gambler," Margaret said, leaning toward her.

Mary laughed. "I'll take that bet."

The court's mood shifted as spring shifted into summer. No one was complaining of the rising heat or the threat of plague. No one fled to their country estates. Everyone was too busy watching the queen, who carried her head high, a hand to her growing belly. Anne Boleyn had told the king she was with child and had felt it quicken in her belly. She went around demanding every respect due to a queen and more. The French envoys and ambassadors hedged their bets and renewed their support of Anne.

The king was eager to placate her. He was certain this was a sign of God's favour and ordered the trials of Sir Thomas More and Bishop Fisher to commence without delay.

Judge and jury knew the outcome the king desired, but it had still taken a lot of bribing and convincing to have both men declared guilty of treason. These were godly, powerful men with the support of the pope, but in the end the jury bowed to pressure.

Everyone at court waited for the king to pardon them and send them home in disgrace. When he didn't, they decided he was just teaching them a lesson, keeping them in the tower for another season or two.

Overseas, Rome was quiet, as far as anyone could tell. Perhaps they were outraged, or perhaps they were calling the king's bluff. They couldn't imagine he would execute a bishop. Sir Francis Bryan slipped back into court as if he had never been gone. Only the slight tan gave him away.

Mary had begun new projects and dreams of her own. She had continued to add to her notebook. But she was loath to circulate it. Instead, she had been busy making copies of certain poems, sharing them around the court. She started to dream bigger of seeing poems printed and distributed all over Europe.

But to see this through she needed a poet like Thomas Wyatt. She took the risk and sent him an encoded message to meet her in the gardens when all the court would be distracted.

Mary, dressed in an unassuming russet gown, waited by a fountain half hidden by large shrubs. She had laid aside her rich headdress, so from afar she might be mistaken for a lady-in-waiting and not a duchess.

She blamed Mary Shelton for making her so daring, and if she got caught then she would never speak to her again. Months at this court filled with indiscretion had made her feel invincible. The rules had changed. It wasn't like in Queen Katherine's day when their behaviour had to be impeccable and they spent their days at prayer, charity work, or needlework.

They enjoyed a lively court that even France

envied.

Mary was lost in her thoughts, so she had been too distracted to notice Wyatt appear. But now she saw him from the corner of her eye.

He was close to her. She could feel his breath on the nape of her neck. His hand rested lightly on her forearm. It sent a tantalising shiver over her skin. She thought for a moment what it would be like to let him take her here and now. But the threat of her father and brother hung over her head. She was not a mere knight's daughter like her Shelton cousin. She had a reputation to uphold. Her work was more important than a moment of ecstasy.

She turned around, stepping away from him as she did so. To her pleasure, he took a step forward as though he was about to reach out and catch her.

"What are you thinking, sir?"

He cocked his head to the side, considering her. Mary met his gaze with a bold one of her own. She was a Howard. She had nothing to fear from someone like him.

When he spoke, his tone was sultry. "If you wish me to go, you simply have to command me."

She caught an edge of amusement to his words. She recalled a line from one of his poems. "Was one never yet of your love grieved?"

His eyes twinkled with surprise, but he didn't hesitate to fling back, "I thought thee true without exception. But I perceive I lacked discretion."

"You do indeed, but I don't think we are so in love we can cause harm to each other," she said with a nod.

He laughed, a clear melodious sound. Mary could see why so many women melted at his feet and words. "I didn't think you admired my work, so I am surprised you memorised it. Have I misjudged the situation? You asked to see me in private, and yet here you are rejecting me by throwing my own poetry at me."

"And that is what I wished to speak to you about: your words," she said, clearing her throat. Her desire vanished as she thought of what she wanted to ask him.

"Ah, so you have summoned me for business," he said with a wink and took a seat on the grass, still damp from morning dew, not caring that it would ruin the rich velvet cloth he wore. Mary almost expected him to invite her to sit beside him, but he simply sat, staring up at her with those large dark eyes of his. He reminded her of a content cat languishing in the early morning sun.

She paced before him, wondering how to begin.

"I wish to see your work published. It would be a shame for it to be lost or forgotten," she said.

"That's what makes it all the more exciting."

Despite his quip, she could see she had captured his attention. He watched her more carefully.

"I have the funds," she said. "But I thought I should also have your permission."

He inclined his head, a smile stretching across his features. "Thoughtful of you, my lady. What would your family say about your endeavours? There would be talk. Already you have taken a risk."

Mary looked at the sky reflected in the water of the fountain. Yes, she was a fool.

"If there's no risk, there's no gain," she said tightly. "I need this."

"Why?"

The question was so innocent but struck something deep within her. Why did she love poetry so much she was willing to stake her reputation on it? Hadn't she always sworn there was nothing more important than her reputation?

They were running out of time. They couldn't dawdle here for long. She had a few explanations, none of them pleasant or easy to share. Her mind whirring, she settled on one that was halfway between truth and shame.

"I told someone once that poetry has the power to invoke emotion, but that is only half the miracle," she said. "A poem has the power to construct a world where only truth resides. In the moment of reading or listening, the writer bares their soul to whoever stumbles across their work. How can I not try to preserve those precious words that strung together create such powerful responses?"

Thomas Wyatt listened attentively. She was grateful he didn't laugh. At last he inclined his head again, piercing her with that intent dark gaze of his.

"Very well, my lady. I consent," he said. "You may

use my work as you please. I don't have a fortune at my disposal to circulate my work or have it printed in a book. I have other demands on my time as well."

"I heard you are to be sent to France," she admitted.

"Ah, is that why your request was so urgent?" He smiled at some private joke.

"And you will keep this secret?" She was desperate to make him swear.

"I haven't been very open with my secret dealings in the past," he said, getting to his feet and brushing himself off. "I'll keep this one for you. But if you'd let me give you some advice, perhaps you need some love in your life. Poetry shouldn't be such an obsessive pastime. It might burn you."

Mary didn't know what to make of this. She was sure he was teasing her, but his expression was serious.

"I know something of what it is to be in a loveless marriage." The explanation came at last with a small shrug.

"Mine isn't a true one," she said in a whisper. "Legally, I suppose it is."

He looked at her with pity in his eyes.

She left before he managed to say something that would draw tears from her eyes. She hated showing weakness, and she couldn't be entirely sure he wouldn't laugh.

At the end of summer, serving women and doctors were rushing in and out from the queen's rooms. Mary was there in the presence chamber, watching wide-eyed as they poured in.

At last Mary Boleyn came out pale and strained, carrying a bloodied bundle of linen. That was when everyone knew. All the midwives, doctors, and prayers for intercession had failed to save the baby in the queen's womb.

The court was quiet. No one knew what to say or how to act. The king had flung himself into work, doing his best to ignore the pitying looks. It was clear to everyone that he was in a dark mood, despite his attempts at cheerfulness. A tournament planned for the following week was cancelled and nothing more was said of it. He took a small hunting party of his favourite attendants and rode out.

With an absent king the palace felt empty. The ladies of the queen's chambers wasted the day away indoors, alternating between praying, reading, and staring glumly out the window.

So Mary was surprised by the summons to come to her father's rooms. As she left the room, she could feel Anne Boleyn's gaze following her on the way out and she had no idea why.

If she hadn't been lost in her own thoughts, perhaps she would have noticed every other Howard lady was missing too.

CHAPTER 6

M ary was agog at the words coming out of her father's mouth. The Howards, most of the Boleyns, and Sheltons were all there. She met her uncle's eyes for reassurance, but he looked away from her.

"What went wrong, then?" He put the question to the room as if he hadn't just accused Anne of being a witch a moment ago.

She realised in a moment of horror they were all looking at her and Mary Shelton. Her father tapped a finger on the walnut table, impatient. He was expecting a reply.

"Nothing, as far as I could tell," Mary said, finding her voice. Her cousin was shaking beside her. "She took ill and then there was nothing for us to do. What could we have done?" She flung the question back at her father with the slightest hint of challenge.

He frowned at her but turned his gaze from her to Mary Shelton, who was busy fiddling with her fingers.

"And you? Did you see nothing?"

"No, Your Grace." Her voice was small, as if she wanted to shrink within herself.

Mary wanted to give her a sign of reassurance, but at this moment it felt like they were being interrogated.

At last Mary Shelton's mother spoke, breaking the uncomfortable silence.

"Women lose babies all the time. She has given the king Princess Elizabeth. This was a mishap. She will bear other children. There's no reason she would not." Her voice rang clear through the room.

The cloud of dread in the room dispersed. She had shown them the light.

Mary watched her father considering before giving them a curt nod.

"Very well," the duke said. "We shall see what the next few weeks bring. It's hard to predict where the king's mood will take him."

The rest of the meeting was a blur for Mary, and she returned to her own apartments to rest rather than go to wait upon the queen. She didn't think anyone would mind right now given the circumstances.

In the end, two things saved Anne Boleyn.

First, the pope had sent overtures to Henry demanding he apologise for his misdeeds and threatening him once again with war. This was backed by Emperor Charles, who threatened to come with his great army to place Katherine back in her rightful place.

Second, Anne, tormented and sick, began to spin the tale that it was Katherine of Aragon's ill-wishing that made her lose the baby. Everyone knew the evil eye was effective at causing miscarriages. The life of a child in the womb was so fragile that it didn't take much to dislodge it.

Supporters of reform and the Boleyns believed it because it suited them and because the Spanish queen continued to defy the king. She wasn't the sort of woman to accept her exile quietly. She had ridden out to battle against the Scots. Now she was turning on her own adoptive country. She must be plotting to find a way for the emperor to conquer England. She was certainly encouraging him. After a while, even her supporters couldn't deny it anymore. They turned their backs on her, afraid of the war she might bring upon them. Her continued defiance was beginning to make her look like a greedy, grasping woman.

Why didn't she just give up? She was causing trouble, and for what? Try as she might, Mary couldn't guess. If she had been Katherine, she would have agreed to the divorce but negotiated to have the best terms. Better to be a rich abbess somewhere than a discarded woman in exile.

By autumn, the king and Anne were friends again. He had no choice but to double down on the path he had chosen to take. Parliament had already declared him head of the church, and money was pouring into his coffers as the tithes that would have been paid to Rome were diverted to him. Maybe he didn't love Anne as he used to, but to give her up now would be to admit he had been wrong. He would have to go back to Katherine, and that he would not do.

The country was readying for a foreign war, but it was clear the general population was unhappy. Change was never easy and to see local monasteries being torn down for the king's profit didn't sit well with them. They saw Anne as a witch leading the king into sin. However, they couldn't support the Spanish either. It was anyone's guess if rebellions would spring up. The country was at a standstill as they waited to see which way the tide would flow.

The local gentry ordered to fortify their fortresses, built outposts to keep a lookout for an invading army. The northern border was patrolled frequently to prevent the Scots from marching over the border. Finally, a small force was sent to Ireland to quell the uprisings. The last thing anyone wanted was an easy harbour from where the French or Spanish might launch an invasion.

Then there was nothing to do but wait.

Even with the holiday season approaching, the mood at court was strained. Everyone was smiling and laughing, but they were hollow acts like those performed by play actors.

Mary was wishing herself away. Even her work

meticulously copying out Wyatt's poems couldn't take her mind off it.

One day she found herself preparing her part for the pageant in an abandoned gallery lit by dim tallow candles. Joyce was with her, sitting on a stool trying to pick apart the poorly done embroidery on a silk scarf without ruining the fabric.

Mary kept forgetting her lines. She was supposed to be Diana, goddess of the hunt, a bit tongue in cheek considering Diana had never been married. But the queen had brushed aside her concerns.

"You are a virgin, aren't you? At the very least you can play the part," Anne Boleyn said.

Mary hadn't been sure if she was trying to insult her or was accusing her of something.

She was muttering curses under her breath when a door opened and a pair of demons and three knights came bursting through, making a racket loud enough to wake the dead.

Mary had been stunned, frozen in place. She knew these were men of the court in costume, but the other-worldly vision made her gasp.

At the sound of her voice they all stopped to look. They were just as surprised to see her there as she was to be interrupted by them. One of them stepped forward, his head inclined, empty hand outstretched as if to show he meant no harm.

"Excuse me, Lady, we didn't mean to startle you. We came here to practice our parts," he said.

She thought the voice sounded familiar behind his visor.

"I thought the same." She indicated the bow she had tossed aside. Then smiled. "If any of you gentlemen would wish to assist me, I need a target for my roses to strike. I haven't yet managed to figure out how to shoot flowers with a bow."

One man snorted.

Mary shrugged. "It is not I who picked this pageant."

"I will volunteer," the knight said.

The others behind him shared glances.

But Mary, filled with mischief, accepted his help. "Stand twenty paces back. That should be sufficient."

Joyce, the voice of caution, placed a hand on her shoulder. "Are you sure you want to do this?"

Mary shook her off. "There's no harm. We are practicing. You are here. What harm could there be?"

Joyce stepped back.

The knight stood there waiting, the others a few paces behind him watching eagerly as Mary picked up her bow. It was the delicate sort made for the women of the court. But she knew they could be just as deadly as a crossbow if the archer was strong enough.

She took her position, a seriousness in her eyes, and notched her bow. She waited, holding the bow taut. There was an intake of breath. Mary knew she was a striking unearthly figure in this dim light, dressed in a gown of silver tissue crowned with antler horns and a crescent moon. She aimed and fired the paper rose. It travelled no farther than an arm's span from her feet.

The room devolved into laughter.

"You see, I am hopeless," she called out over the noise.

The knight approached, picking up the rose. He lifted his visor and Mary recognised Charles Blount hiding underneath that costume. He was examining the rose as intently as she was studying him.

"This will never fly far. You should ask a fletcher to design you an arrow that will resemble a rose rather than force a rose to take the shape of an arrow."

"That would spoil the symbolism," she said, plucking it from his hands. "Thank you, Master Blount, for your advice. I'll let the queen know. I suppose we can throw them by hand. Even though I like the bow."

"You are supposed to be the Goddess Diana?" he asked.

She nodded.

"Good luck then." He turned and looked at his compatriots. "Let's find another hidden passage to practice in."

Mary watched him herd them out. He was far too serious to be a young man at this court.

That evening, as they took up their positions before the watching court, she felt she had embodied the role. They had waited for the sun to dip over the horizon, and only a few candles were lit around the hall, casting a soft glow on the stage. There were three parts to this tableau. When it came time for her to spring bare-footed among the trees, she remembered her lines and, though she was still emotionless in her delivery, performed better than others.

A great stag sprang up and she, after a moment of feigned surprise, lifted her bow to strike. Since they had not yet figured out a way to make the rose fly, she threw it as gracefully as she could manage. With a thump it hit the stag, which crumpled to the ground behind a conveniently placed bush. A second later, a knight sprang up. The stag had been a man all along. She ran. Diana always ran from men. Mary moved back among the trees and disappeared from view, even as the knight called out a pining verse of love and grati-tude for breaking the spell.

She waited for the play to end and then came out with all the players to bow before the applauding royal couple. The king awarded a gold rose to the goddess Venus, who just so happened to be Mary Shelton, and a golden cup to the best of the knights.

They bowed again, expressing their gratitude before shuffling away. Servants came forth to clear out the rest of the scenery to make room for the next performance. A troupe of jugglers and fools.

Mary changed back into a gown of tawny velvet trimmed with black fur. She emerged, dressed like a royal duchess once more. Charles Blount was a few steps ahead of her, heading back to the great hall. She called out to him and he turned to see her.

"You are yourself again," he said with a smile.

"I am." She strode forward. "It feels good to set aside the trappings of a goddess who spends her time running in the woods."

He looked pensive. "Yes, it must get incredibly lonely." He returned her smile and then offered her his arm. "Shall I escort you back to your seat?"

She took a step away from him. "No, go ahead of me. I'll wait for my cousin."

He tipped his head to her and continued on his way. She watched him go, wistfully imagining she had accepted. Being around him was like sitting before a warm fire on a cold day. Relaxing and soothing. His blue eyes were filled with warmth and understanding. But Mary thought she was just imagining things. He was simply unlike the other men at court, who were all pushing and shoving each other to show their prowess in one area or another. Mary enjoyed her uncle's humour, Wyatt's wit, Sir Francis Bryan's mystery, and the king's power.

But Charles Blount was far more interesting to try to puzzle out, an enigma who refused to be a lover, a politician, or a fighter. As far as she could tell, he was simply himself.

They were huddled in the alcove together, trying to be as inconspicuous as possible as they passed paper back and forth.

"No." She shook her head. "This would not suit the theme."

"What is the theme? You don't seem to have a strict plan in mind."

She swatted Thomas Wyatt but hit him harder than she intended to. He let out a yelp, and she almost clamped her hand over his mouth to stifle his cry.

Luckily, the sound had been hidden by the lute player's song.

"Shh," she said but shot him an apologetic grin. "If you must know, I thought the theme could be loss."

"Not very creative," he said, teasing her.

She wasn't one to tolerate his criticism. Most people let him get away with anything, either because they were in awe of his skills or his looks. He had good connections and always weaselled his way out of any trouble. Mary had heard enough tales of his drinking and whoring to know this man was no saint but had the luck of one. She saw his skill as something entirely separate from his being. "Then you should be more diverse in what you write."

"You strike me again." Thomas Wyatt placed a hand over his heart feigning hurt.

"If you start crying, I might for real," she said, clearing her throat as she considered a fresh pile of papers. When he was silent for too long, she looked up to see him studying her with that intent dark gaze.

"What would it take for you to fall in love? I would greatly like to see it. You claw at me until I give up my words and you use them to warm your icy heart, but perhaps you just need a bit of kissing."

She was tempted to kick him. Predicting she would, he moved out of reach. "Lady Ice, I trust your judgment in this. Forgive my teasing."

She rolled her eyes but said nothing more by way of response and then he was gone. His attention caught by some brown-eyed beauty that he preferred these days.

Mary Shelton came rushing by with Henry Norris on her arm. She stopped short to see Mary alone in the alcove, trying to reorder the poems to her liking.

"Why aren't you having some fun?" she asked.

"I am," Mary corrected her but tried to reassure her. "I promise, and what about you?"

Her cousin flushed pink. "We are—getting some fresh air," she said with a laugh.

"Don't let anyone catch you," Mary said, not that she thought it mattered much. Everyone knew that Mary Shelton had been the king's mistress for a time. If she had any reputation left to protect, it was gone now.

Her cousin leaned in close to whisper in her ear. "He told me he loves me. Truly loves me. He wishes to marry me. He will speak to my father soon."

"I am happy for you," Mary said with a twinge of jealousy. "Truly."

Mary Shelton squeezed her hand and was gone.

She was left alone with her papers. Maybe Wyatt was right; she needed some love in her life. But that was foolish to wish for.

Mary had not known at the time, but that had been the beginning of the end of the carefree days at court. That summer the king, in a fury, signed the death warrants for both Fisher and More. They were spared a traitor's death but were marched out before a crowd and beheaded by one stroke of the axe.

Mary had been there. Her husband had been there. Anyone who wished to make it clear to the king they weren't standing against him had been there. It didn't matter that hardly anyone actually thought these men deserved such a grisly end. Bishop Fisher was so old and frail. He had served as confessor to the king's grandmother, the famously pious Margaret Beaufort. For what it was worth, he met his end bravely without a shadow of fear.

When the executioner held up his head to proclaim that here died a traitor, Mary thought he looked serene, with the ghost of a smile on his lips. Her stomach churned at the sight of all that blood, and she looked away to her husband. He was pale, but his face was determined, as if he was forcing himself to look. She knew he hadn't been eager to attend the executions. But he feared appearing weak more and it strengthened his resolve.

She wondered if this was his first execution. It certainly had not been hers. When she was a child she had been brought to the tower to see her grandfather, the Duke of Buckingham, be executed. She had once seen a heretic burn too. That had been the worst. The wood had been wet and the man had choked to death on smoke. She tried to shake the memories from her head.

It was best not to dwell on such matters for long.

Even after the deaths of these two men, the queen's appetite for blood was not sated, and Mary wouldn't be surprised if the court was here again in due time. It was an open secret that Anne Boleyn had begun pressuring the king to do something about Katherine of Aragon and her daughter. She didn't have the same influence over the king that she had a year ago, but on this matter the king was willing to listen. Only the Spanish ambassador with his threats of war and his cautious privy council were able to keep them from being brought to trial.

No one was in a mood to celebrate that Christmas, not even when the queen missed her courses for the second time. They had learned hope was futile until there was a living child in the cradle. Anne Boleyn left off her gambling and frivolities and began spending her days in prayer and contemplation. Still the pressure on the king to bring his previous wife and daughter to justice never relented.

In the end, it didn't matter. Katherine of Aragon obliged Anne by dying. She breathed her last on a cold winter January day. She died stubborn as a mule, calling herself Queen of England. Mary wondered if the king punished her for this last rebellion by having her buried without ceremony in Peterborough Cathedral. Her daughter had not been allowed to attend the funeral, but many other noble ladies risked the hard road to pay her homage.

Mary was in an anxious mood. A secret was gnawing at her as she helped Anne dress each day.

Her father had heard that the king was wondering if his marriage to Anne was a true one. He grilled her one evening on the queen's behaviour, making a note of everything she said. But then after the queen shared her happy news, the duke dropped the matter. Mary couldn't help but wonder for how long.

Without knowing it, Anne had conceived just in time. The king wouldn't move against her, not when she could be carrying an heir in her belly. Mary wasn't sure why Anne was so blind to the king's increasing disinterest and annoyance with her. The passion he had once been so dazzled by exhausted him now. But Anne's temper never seemed to cool long enough for her to see the danger she was putting herself in.

Both Anne Boleyn and the king were in a celebratory mood following Katherine's funeral. They wore yellow and danced as if death was cause for celebration.

In a way it was, but neither was celebrating the same thing.

Anne had seen Katherine as a threat, secretly fearing that the king might return to his first wife, so now she smiled and laughed, thinking she was safe at last. Meanwhile, the king sang a happy tune because Katherine's death meant the threat of Spanish invasion was lifted, and if he wished he could set Anne aside for another bride. A younger, more fertile one.

❧

Mary handed Margaret Douglas a heavy furred mitt. The king had announced a tournament, and he would be riding in the lists. Not wishing to ruin his good mood, no one dared to tell him this was distasteful.

Anne Boleyn, sick in the morning, remained behind in her rooms, safe and warm, holding back only a few ladies to keep her company. The rest of them were to go watch. Mary would have preferred to stay behind, but Margaret was keen to go.

"It's been so long since we've had any fun," Margaret said. "Won't it be exciting? All those brave knights."

Mary had laughed. "Is there one in particular you are thinking of?"

Margaret blushed but said nothing for a while. "I'm simply looking forward to a bit of fun. It's a welcome change at court, even if this all feels wrong."

Mary nodded. "It does feel like we are celebrating someone's death. Even if that someone was a traitor to England." She said the words in case anyone overheard and reported them. They always spoke like this about such weighty matters, even when they thought they were alone. People had been placed under suspicion for much less. A slip of the tongue and calling Mary Tudor "princess" could land your name on some list. Your household would be questioned. Then one day you would wake up to find yourself arrested and heading to the block.

Behind all of this was Thomas Cromwell, who did the king's bidding with ruthless efficiency. In the early days of Anne Boleyn's rise he had always been in her rooms, doing whatever she required. Then, as time went on, he ingratiated himself with the king and became indispensable. Despite his low birth, he had become his principal adviser and for good reason. Give Thomas Cromwell a shilling and by the end of the day he would have turned it into a tidy fortune. Indeed, the dissolution of the monasteries had brought the king untold wealth.

Though her father grumbled and cursed Cromwell under his breath, he still bought up church land, increasing his income significantly.

If her husband was at all inclined to listen to her,

Mary would have pressured him to do the same. He was living as grandly as a prince, showered with honours and riches beyond his actual status. Should a prince be born in holy wedlock, he would find his position greatly diminished. Instead of relying on his father for his wealth, he should build it up himself.

But no one was listening to her. No one cared that she thought it served the nobles right for being slack in their jobs when other hungrier and more ambitious men came and snatched them away.

Margaret and Mary dressed warmly in fur-lined gowns and heavy stockings. The men would be riding in the field under arm, adrenaline coursing through their veins, but they would be watching from the pavilions.

The jousts began to great fanfare.

Mary watched her uncle and George Boleyn face off in an even match. They were both unhorsed, but George Boleyn won in the end.

Across the field, sitting among the men, she spotted the familiar blue eyes of Charles Blount. Mary was surprised he was not riding. Even those who knew they had no chance at winning or couldn't afford the expense borrowed armour and horses to make a brief appearance. It was a matter of honour and getting the chance to catch the attention of the king was priceless. So why was he sitting back among the men too old or injured to ride?

The games proceeded with brief interludes for the

field to be raked and the participants to catch their breath.

Then it was the king's turn. They weren't supposed to know it was the king. That was part of the fun, but despite the heavy armour and visor hiding his face, there wasn't a man in England as broad and tall as him.

Everyone was so focused on him they weren't even paying attention to his opponent. Steam was rising from his great charger as he held a tight grip on his lance. The horn blew and the horse raced forward, kicking up a cloud of dust.

The next moment, a terrible scream filled the air. The king's horse was flat on the ground, the king trapped beneath him. Mary must have blinked. When did this happen? How did this happen?

All at once cries arose from the gathered crowd. They all moved toward the struggling horse and the silent king.

Was he dead? Mary, caught up in the emotion, ran forward. Watching as the king's body was dragged away from the horse by several men.

A hand gripped her forearm, pulling her along. She looked up to see her father's grim determined face. He didn't say a word to her, and she didn't resist.

He pushed past the men crowding the entrance of the tent.

The king was on a great table. They were slowly removing his armour, which looked dented. His eyes were closed and his mouth slightly open, and she thought for one horrid moment he was dead. But then her father released a breath.

"Alive, then?"

The man unbuckling the king's shin straps nodded. Mary wondered how her father had known, but of course he was more familiar with death than she was.

"Has someone sent for the doctor?" the Duke of Suffolk asked, kneeling by his friend's side but too scared to touch him.

Other questions were thrown around. Chaos was spreading through the tent, and even though they could see the king was still breathing, he had not woken nor responded.

Her father shouted for silence, taking command of the situation. Mary was grateful for his strength.

"We shall take him back to the palace. Have a cart brought. We must be careful when moving him. We will tell everyone the king is unhurt but has taken a shock and needs to rest," he said.

Thomas Cromwell was at his side, shouting out orders to see that the duke's instructions were followed.

That was when her father turned to her and she noticed he was still gripping her arm.

"You will go to the queen's rooms. Say nothing, but write to your husband and your brother. Tell them to come as soon as they can. They are to stop for nothing and ride with an armed escort."

That was the first time he had referred to Fitzroy as

her husband. She was still trying to make sense of what he was saying when he gave her a little shake.

"Don't say a word to the queen. I will come and tell her shortly. First write the letter. Do you understand me?"

"Yes," she said at last.

He released her then, and she bolted away from the dreadful tent and the sleeping king.

She was making her way to her apartments through Greenwich Palace, when she ran into Mary Shelton carrying a few books.

"Mary? What is wrong?" she asked, her face clouded by concern.

Mary shook her head. "I cannot say. I must go."

"You look like you are about to faint." Mary Shelton wasn't smiling, despite her light teasing tone. "I'm coming with you."

Mary didn't argue but pressed on down the corridors and past the guards stationed at her doors. For now the palace was quiet, but it wouldn't be for long. She had to hurry.

In a hurried hand she wrote two letters, signed and sealed them, hoping the ink had dried and wouldn't smudge. She commanded her steward to send a trusted page to ride to Richmond in all haste. She pressed a gold coin into his hand and he promised he wouldn't fail her.

Then she collapsed back in her chair.

Mary Shelton had seen some of what she wrote.

She came over with a cup of wine and waited for her to drink it dry.

"The king might be..." Even she couldn't finish the thought.

Mary nodded. "But no one thinks so. He took a nasty fall. You must swear you won't say anything."

Her cousin promised, and then after a long moment of contemplation looked at her with awe. "Your father is moving to secure the throne, should anything happen."

Mary shrugged, as if it had nothing to do with her, until she realised what she had just done. Yes, of course her father, who was loyal to nothing but the throne, would be working to secure it, but for whom? That was the question.

She swallowed hard, looking down at her ink-stained hands. It might just be her husband that he would back. He wouldn't be keen on leaving Anne in charge—they had been quarrelling—and Princess Elizabeth was just a girl. Mary Tudor had been disinherited and was currently under house arrest. So that left Fitzroy as the next viable heir, assuming her father could get the backing of the privy council. Considering Anne Boleyn had made an enemy of most of them, it would not be hard to do. Their only other options were even less suited for the task. Mary listed them all by name in her head, mostly women or other disinherited heirs. She thought of what a terror Fitzroy would be if he was made king now. Mary said a silent prayer for the king's recovery.

"We must return to the queen," Mary Shelton said, her face set in a serious determination so unlike her usual cheerful countenance.

"Don't say anything to her," Mary said to her cousin. "We must think of her child."

As they walked into the queen's room arm in arm, they saw a nightmarish sight. Mary's father, the Duke of Norfolk, stood before a weeping mass of fabric and skirts that contained the queen of England. The two ladies on either side of her were trying to get her to her feet, urging her to be calm, while she continued to wail.

Clearly, no one had bothered to warn her father to be careful how he delivered the news. Or perhaps that had been his intention. Mary wished she could be certain her father wasn't a monster.

CHAPTER 7

The darkness was all-consuming. Mary fought against the urge to sneeze at the heavy scent of incense and cleansing herbs in the air.

She waited as her eyes adjusted and she could make out the bed. The curtains were drawn tight around it. Five ladies sat at the foot of the bed on stools waiting for any word from within. Where were the rest of them? Anne Boleyn's retinue was large, far larger than Katherine of Aragon's had been.

Mary wanted to flee this miserable room, the stink of death and misery in every corner.

One lady, Anne Stanhope, turned to look at her with a blank quizzical look that seemed to say *why are you here?*

Mary approached, bowing to the bed that held the ailing queen as custom dictated. Anne Boleyn had lost her baby, a prince that never breathed. The tiny half-formed body had been carried out of the room and buried somewhere. That had been a day ago. Three days since her father had given her a shock that sent her into a panic.

She could see by the looks on the women's faces that still the king had not come. Not because he was ill or dead but because he felt utterly betrayed by his wife and wanted nothing more to do with her. He had taken a terrible fall and had been at death's door. Angry at his own mortality, he lashed out at the first person to disappoint him, and that was Anne.

Mary took a seat beside them, joining their silent vigil. As she sat there, her mind churned and she touched the rosary beads tied at her waist. She hadn't seen or spoken to her father since the day of the king's fall. She was scared to know what he might say. Mary remembered her uncle calling after her as she rode away, telling her she wasn't paying attention. He had been talking about poetry then and the power of words. She should have considered that it could be applied to court life as well.

Somewhere along the line her father had withdrawn his support from the Boleyn queen and she hadn't noticed. Was it after Anne had insulted him one too many times? Or when he lost faith in her ability to give the king a son? What possessed him to tell her that the king might be dead in such a blunt and horrible way? Had he wanted to do her some harm? He couldn't have known for certain that the news he gave her that day would cause her to miscarry, but he must have known it was a possibility. She remembered the stories about him and her mother. They said he had dragged her from childbed by the hair. It was such an outrageous tale that no one believed it, but now Mary thought it might have happened. She shivered. Her father's stoic ruthlessness had always been comforting to her. He was a great general and defender of the realm, keeping her safe. He quelled rebellions at great personal loss to keep the throne secure. But now she saw how quickly he could turn around and strike the very people he had been protecting. What if he turned on her too? He couldn't. He wouldn't.

A noise from behind the bed curtains jolted her from her thoughts.

"Where is Henry? Where is the king?"

They pushed back the curtains and rushed to comfort the queen, urging her to drink warm broth and take a cup of mulled ale.

She was unbearably frail, covered up in heavy blankets and furs, her hair tied neatly in a cap. She looked so small.

But then her dark eyes fixated on Mary and she glared.

"Where is the duke, my uncle?"

"In council," someone answered.

Anne frowned at this. "And the king?"

"We will tell him you have awoken."

Anne nodded. A look of fear passed over her eyes. "He has not left? He will come?"

"Yes, yes," they all reassured her.

Mary knew what she was fearing. King Henry VIII had left his first wife and never returned. He could do the same with her.

At length the king did come. The ladies had strived to make Anne presentable. She was still weak and shaking from the loss of her child, but she gathered her strength and put on a brave show.

He asked after her health and said all the things a husband should say on such an occasion. Mary followed his every move and she could see he was barely able to maintain eye contact with his wife. When he did look at her, there was no warmth in his gaze.

Now, ten minutes after his arrival, he was already looking to leave. Anne called out in a final moment of desperation. He stopped and she reached out to him.

"Henry, we will have another child. It was that witch that cursed my womb, but now she is gone and no one stands in our way. You must believe this."

Mary watched the expression on the king's face darken.

"Rest, Anne," he said before leaving.

The queen was shocked to find her husband gone so fast. After Elizabeth's birth he had come and stayed by her side, feeding her sweetmeats and sponging her forehead. When she had lost her other child he had stayed at her side and they consoled each other.

Now it was clear he wanted nothing more to do with her. He couldn't stand being in her presence.

Mary looked around the room. The attendants and servants were all fixing their eyes on the floor. The ladies were stepping away from the queen, wishing themselves away.

It might all have been forgotten in a season or two, but events got out of hand.

Rumours began circulating that Anne had given birth to a monster. The king was beginning to express doubts about the validity of his marriage to her and was not keeping it secret. Soon everyone in the city was certain Anne was a witch that had seduced the king.

Then Jane Seymour, that plain sow-faced girl with dull blue eyes, was moved into private apartments near the king. Mary recalled how she and Mary Shelton had often made fun of her. Now, by some miracle she had the king's favour. If there were any witchcraft going on at court, Mary would look in that quarter.

Anne's power was slipping away. She found herself alone. A sad shell of her former self. Anne acted as if nothing had happened. She acted as if she might quicken with child soon despite her husband never visiting her bed these days. She prayed more fervently and began to keep that fiery temper in check. It wasn't enough.

Whatever had drawn people to her in the past was gone. She was nothing more than a falling star.

It was like something out of a dream when the king's men came for her.

In May, Mary was packing away the cloak Anne had worn at the joust in a thick oak chest. She heard the sound of feet tramping in. By this point she was numb with fatigue and when she saw the armed guards she could only blink. Someone was at her side, pulling her away. She fought, remembering the day her father had pulled her into that accursed tent.

"Peace, niece." He released her.

She looked up to see her uncle's serene face looking down at her. "Come away. This is no place for you," he whispered.

He was leading her toward a side door through which they might slip away. Anne had caught the movement.

"Where are you going, Lady Mary? I did not dismiss you."

"You will pardon her, Your Grace," her uncle said, smoothly stepping in front of her. "Her father has summoned her to his side."

The queen looked like she wanted to argue that she was queen. Her desires had precedence over a duke's, but she must have realised that she had bigger fights ahead of her.

Mary and her uncle dropped into their respective curtsies and bows and left the room.

He didn't stop until they were safe behind Howard doors.

"What is happening?" Mary asked him after he deposited her on an upholstered divan.

"She is to be questioned by the privy council and" —he paused, as if he couldn't believe what he was about to say— "more than likely she will be arrested and taken to the tower."

Mary gasped. She was no fan of Anne Boleyn's, but the thought of a queen of England arrested seemed ludicrous to her. She wanted to ask for what, but her uncle continued.

"Your father wanted you out of the way. The ladies of her household will be questioned, but he wants you to have no part of it."

Selfishly pleased she would be excluded, she relaxed. It no longer felt like her heart was caught in her throat. Her uncle was pouring them wine from her father's cupboard.

His hand trembled slightly as he held it out to her.

She wondered why he was so stricken by the news.

"What are you not telling me?" she asked, looking at the blood-red liquid in her cup.

"At least three men are under arrest. They are suspected of cuckolding the king," he said at last.

"Anne is accused of taking lovers?" She was genuinely surprised. She thought that—well, it didn't matter what she thought, not really.

"Yes." He was avoiding looking at her.

"Tell me with who. You wouldn't be suspected, would you?" she asked.

"No." He shook his head. "But Henry Norris is among the men taken to the tower."

"No!" Mary exclaimed. "There must be some mistake. He's head over heels in love with Mary. They have probably become involved in some scheme to marry in secret. It's not the queen he writes poetry to."

"I don't think it matters much." His voice was strained. "She should be grateful she hasn't been accused of far worse. But Thomas Cromwell and your uncle have it in hand. The old families of England have banded together against her. She is to be a great whore, nothing more."

"He will divorce her then," Mary said, thinking for Anne that was a fate worse than death.

"If not more," her uncle said, a faraway look in his eye.

He left her to her own devices, instructing her not to leave these apartments.

She wondered how this all came to pass.

The rest of the month was like walking through a strange dream. After Mary Shelton had been examined and cross-examined, she came to cry in her arms.

"They will kill him," she sobbed. "They will kill

my Henry. And there is nothing I can do. I tried to explain..." she trailed off.

It wasn't only Henry Norris who was facing the headsman.

The following day Mary heard that Thomas Wyatt had been taken to the tower as well. The rumours about him and Anne were old. Even if they were true, why should he be called a traitor now? The king had never even known about Anne back then.

Mary couldn't imagine him in a cell. She fussed around her rooms, unable to stand feeling so useless. She was determined to find some way to help him. He was a gentleman and wouldn't be mishandled by his guards, but that didn't mean he would have comforts.

She was too much of a coward to ask her father for help on his behalf, but a day later a fresh plan had formed in her mind. Before her fear could take over, she packed herself, Joyce, and a man in her employ into a barge.

At the tower Kingston himself came out to greet her.

"Lady Mary." He bowed respectfully. "What can I help you with?"

Mary sighed, as if she would rather not be here, and pointed to the parcels Joyce and the broad-shouldered Timothy were carrying.

"I am to deliver some linen and other necessities to the queen," she said. "If it is not too much trouble. May I be escorted to her rooms?"

"You need not trouble yourself," Kingston said. "I can have my men bring them to her."

Mary smiled, grateful. "That would be wonderful, but I was asked to see them delivered myself."

"Very well," Kingston said. "I shall escort you myself."

Mary's mind was whirling as she tried to think of an excuse, but she was saved by the arrival of an urgent messenger from court.

"I shall ask Stephen to escort you," he said. "Wait right here." She was tempted to run off, but she didn't know the tower and would just as soon get lost. There would be plenty of awkward questions then.

Stephen was a chatty fellow, whose disposition was too cheerful for her to believe he worked at the tower.

"There are many people here," she said offhandedly.

"As I am sure you heard, quite a few were arrested recently," he said, inclining his head.

He wasn't as empty-headed as he appeared to be, Mary thought. Then, saying a prayer, she thought she might as well ask. "If it's not too much to ask, where is Thomas Wyatt kept?"

He pointed a spindly finger to the ceiling. "A few floors above. Why?"

She shifted from one foot to another. Her free hand pulled out a coin from her purse. "Will you take me to him?"

Stephen frowned. "That wouldn't—"

Mary interrupted before he could say no. "It's just that his wife asked me to give him a message. She's terribly distraught. She wants to make sure he's alive and well."

"Why didn't she come here herself?" His frown deepened.

Mary pulled out two more coins. The man's eyes watched her count them out. "She was scared she wouldn't come out again. They have a young son."

"Very well, but only for a few minutes."

She thanked her lucky stars as she handed him the coin. "Thank you for understanding."

He grunted and changed course. Anne was lodging in the royal apartments, but the rest of the men arrested with her were not. They went up a long winding stone staircase. Behind her Joyce was struggling with the packages, and Mary had to ask Stephen for his assistance.

Then, without any more delays, they arrived. It was Stephen who ordered the guards on duty to open the door. Mary stood there arranging her face into a bored expression as if traipsing around the tower was something she did every day.

She stepped inside before anyone could change their mind. Joyce came in with her so no one could accuse her of anything.

Thomas Wyatt was stretched out on a pallet bed, tossing what looked like a ball up into the air and catching it. He jumped to his feet at the first sight of her but tried not to look too surprised when Stephen poked his head in to remind them he could only give them a moment of privacy.

"What on God's earth are you doing here, madam?" he said.

"Madam, is it?" She rolled her eyes. "I think I prefer Lady Ice." She could see now that he had been tossing a crumpled piece of paper into the air.

"We don't have much time. I wanted to bring you some paper and ink, although I see you don't treasure it too much," she said pointedly.

He looked sheepish and hid the ball behind his hand like any child might. Hidden within the folds of her gown, she removed a pouch and handed it to him.

"Paper, ink, a bit of coin to bribe the guards with," she said. "I wanted you to know your book of poems is almost ready for the printers. You must live to hold it in your hands."

"Thank you for this," he said. "You didn't need to risk yourself coming here. Not for me."

She shrugged. "I thought I ought to. You are well?"

"As well as I can be," he said, looking out the thin slit of his window. "I don't do well in captivity."

"I can't imagine many people would." She sighed. "I should go—"

He turned back to her. "Wait. Please do me one last favour. He pulled out a thin sheet of paper he had hidden underneath his jacket. Will you give this to Cromwell? It's for Bess Darrel."

Mary vaguely recognised the name, but what shocked her was that he would have her ask Cromwell for help. "Cromwell? Are you sure?"

"Yes." He pressed the letter into her hands. "Please. I will ask nothing of you ever again."

"I will." She looked sceptical. "He will help you?"

"As best he can, and if not..."

"Bess is your lover?" She couldn't help but ask.

He nodded. "And I need to know she will be looked after—if I were not around."

She nodded. Before she could say anything she heard the door handle turn and she was already saying goodbye to him. Mary didn't bother asking Stephen for more time and let him lead her to Anne Boleyn's rooms.

If the ladies were surprised to find the Duke of Norfolk's daughter delivering linen, they didn't say anything. Most of the room was filled with Howard women. Even little Catherine Carey was there, sitting by the aunt that had her banished from court. She looked too young for such dreary work.

Anne didn't look away from the fireplace she was seated in front of, and Mary didn't dawdle.

On the way out she thanked Kingston for his assistance and left on the waiting barge, happy to get away from the damp tower and the stench that permeated through the air.

A few days later she was walking in the gardens when Sir Francis Bryan approached her, his face grim. She noted that for once he was dressed in muted tones of grey and silver.

"What were you thinking?" he said, shaking his head.

"I don't know what you mean." She walked faster. Mary didn't need to hear how he disapproved of her actions.

"You realise your visit to the tower was noticed," he called after her, not troubling to keep his voice down.

"Pardon me," she hissed, turning around.

"I might as well shout it from the rooftops," he said, throwing his hands up as though he was about to do just that. Then his shoulders slumped and he approached. "I am sorry, but you risked yourself and others with your playacting. You are lucky Kingston came to me first and I covered for you."

Mary squeezed her right hand to stop it from trembling. "He spoke to you?"

"Yes, you dolt." He sighed again, peering down at her with his one eye. There wasn't anything malevolent about him. Otherwise Mary might have real reason to fear.

"So—what now?"

"Now you swear to me you shall never try anything so foolhardy again." He leaned closer to her. "Wyatt has other friends, even family. Let them risk their necks by sending him little gifts. Your father has been protecting you, but he won't if you fall under the shadow of suspicion." He took a deep breath in. "I cannot. I will not do more."

She swallowed hard. His face, usually so jovial and eager, was devoid of all emotion now. This was the other side of him, the mask he wore when he went about doing the king's business. Ruthless, and unscrupulous.

"I understand," she said, her words barely a whisper.

"Good. I bid you a good day then," he said.

After he was gone, Mary's mind drifted to the letter Wyatt had given her. She had promised him to see Cromwell. That would be like walking into the lion's den. She drew in a breath. She had already made her decision. Howards were supposed to be fearless. She would do this one last thing.

Cromwell had some of the best rooms in the palace, close to the king and well furnished, but they looked less like private apartments and more like a place of business. At least three clerks were stationed at desks around the room, going through dispatches. She took a moment to steady herself. Cromwell wasn't some monster out of a fairy story and she wasn't a child. She would have to trust Wyatt when he said he was a friend. She stepped toward the doors. The guards at the door bowed and let her through.

And so she found herself standing in front of the very person her father had tried to keep her away from.

"Lady Mary, what brings you to my humble office?" Cromwell asked.

This room was anything but humble. Every inch was decorated with elaborate paintings and tapestries. Hundreds of candles were lit, burning away a fortune as they filled the room with brilliant light.

"I have a letter for you from Wyatt," she said after a moment's hesitation. Why bother with lies when the truth would sound just as fantastical? She watched him carefully, but he showed no signs of surprise. She assumed he knew already. "He asked me to give it to you. In case—" She couldn't finish.

He waited.

"—it all goes wrong," she coughed.

"I am surprised you didn't come here begging for the queen's life. I suppose you aren't great friends. You must have heard how she tried to poison your husband."

Mary shook her head. No, she had not heard this particular rumour.

"Well, thank you for bringing this to me," Cromwell said, breaking the seal with one hand. "I will do what I can for him."

"Thank you." She curtsied and left the room, not wishing to remain any longer.

She fled down to the stairs and into the gardens, losing herself among the greenery.

"My lady, are you well?"

Mary looked up, blinking back tears. There was

Charles Blount, looking concerned but much the same as he always looked.

"I am quite well," she said to reassure him, but her voice cracked and he looked doubtful.

"Lost a bit too much at gambling?"

She couldn't help but laugh. That would be so much simpler. "No."

"I thought not," he admitted ruefully. "You see, I thought I might cheer you up. I know your cousin and friends are in the tower. I am sorry for you."

"Not for them?"

"I cannot offer them comfort, so it would be useless of me to waste time on the sentiment."

She tilted her head, regarding him. "I never took you for a cold man."

"I like to think of myself as practical. I find I am often too emotional for my own good. But I know when there is no point fighting. Sometimes it's best to conserve energy. Accept things you cannot change and find peace. Otherwise, how can you ever be happy again?"

She remembered then how it was rumoured his father had died of heartbreak over King Henry's decision to break with Rome. The Mountjoys had been staunch Catholics and likely still were.

"Do you believe the king will return to Rome once Anne is gone?" She could see she had surprised him with her forward question. "That is what all the old families think."

"Are you not part of those old families you speak of with such disdain?" He cleared his throat. "But no. I think the king will do as he thinks is right. He is not a changeable man. I pity Anne Boleyn and all those taken up with her. They have been caught in the great political game of the court. Shall I say more and risk indicting myself?" He spoke in that soft way of his.

She hesitated. She was feeling cold even though June was approaching and the sun was high overhead. In a moment of weakness or self-pity she couldn't recall, she looked at him and said, "I am scared."

He nodded. "I think we all are. I should leave you now. Take care, Lady Mary."

⚜

After that little interlude she became more and more aware of his presence at court. She placed herself in his way, contrived ways to bump into him.

He was a balm on her mind, which couldn't believe what was happening. A great court had been convened to try Anne Boleyn for adultery and incest with the men arrested and her own brother.

At night she prayed that Thomas Wyatt and Henry Norris would escape the cruel fate awaiting all traitors. If anything was possible in this mad, mad world, why not mercy?

In her desk the first copy of the printed manuscript

waited to be shown to Wyatt. Would he live long enough to see his work sold at bookshops?

On the day they declared George Boleyn guilty and sentenced him to death she cried alone in an abandoned antechamber. She heard his familiar footsteps before she saw Charles Blount. Like the rest of him, they were soft.

"Lady Mary, where are your lady's maids?" He spoke to her as though he wanted to chide her, but there was nothing amusing about his expression. He looked as miserable as she.

"Sir Blount, don't trouble yourself over me. Go on, leave me to my tears," she said.

He half turned to leave before she reached out to him. Her hand in his. He looked amazed to find it there.

"You aren't supposed to leave," she said. "Have you not read any poetry? This is the part where you wrap me in your arms and—"

She was leaning toward him, craning her neck. Her lips brushed against his, more like a gentle caress than a kiss. Slowly he pulled away.

"You are distressed," he said. "You aren't in your right mind."

She was frozen in place. Surprised at her own daring and hurt by his rejection. "Is it wrong to want a bit of comfort? I am not the first to want it."

He grew more serious at that. "You deserve every comfort, but we are both two married people. It would be a sin to betray the trust of those we have pledged to love."

"My husband does not trouble himself with remaining faithful to me," she said, a pout on her lips.

"But that doesn't give you permission to be forsworn." Charles stepped forward, placing a hand on her shoulder, a comforting gesture but one to keep the distance between them as well. "Don't think that I don't find you desirable. Only a blind man would not see your charms. But you would be endangering yourself, body and soul."

She wanted to argue that plenty of people found comfort outside their marriages. Why should she hold herself to a higher standard? But the fog cleared and she saw more clearly. He wasn't the sort of man that broke his vows. He wasn't like the other courtiers with their sugary words and false smiles. Hadn't that been the reason she noticed him in the first place?

"You won't tell?" she said, hating how piteous she sounded.

"I'll take it to my grave." He touched his lips. "I shall remember the gentle kiss of Diana, who noticed a mere baron of no importance."

She managed a smile and watched as he left. She should have been overwhelmed by embarrassment, but the kind way he had turned her down and his assurance that he wouldn't tell anyone made her relax. What a fool she was.

CHAPTER 8

T he queen was dead.

Her brother and three other gentlemen had paid with their lives to ensure the king had the divorce he wanted.

It was Mary's father that sat as judge for their trial. She wasn't sure how he could sentence his own niece to death, but he had done it. Mary was sure the tears he cried were not over the loss of Anne but for the damage done to the Howard reputation. She hadn't told her fears to anyone, but that didn't make them any less real. She was wary of her own father now.

By some stroke of luck, Thomas Wyatt had managed to keep his head. Or maybe she wasn't giving Cromwell enough credit. Regardless, there was no time to sit around thinking for too long.

Ten days after Anne's execution, the king married Jane Seymour. It had been a small wedding in the queen's chapel and no coronation was planned yet. However, that didn't stop the country from celebrating. Mary attended one feast after another. So she was there to witness the honours heaped on Jane and her family just as they had been on Anne. It was her father who ensured that she was among the prominent ladies in Jane's household. It helped that she was also married to the king's heir apparent. With Princess Elizabeth declared a bastard, there was no one else but him that could be named heir if something were to happen to the king.

For this excellent reason, Fitzroy was brought to court and joined in the celebrations. They never spoke of the letter she sent him and how he had flown to the capital with her brother and fifty armed guards. It had all been forgotten, but he danced with her and gave her a pretty gift.

"Soon we will be allowed to live together as man and wife," he said to her one evening.

She found herself going through the motions. The shy glance, the flush spreading over her cheeks, but everything was to hide the anxiety she felt. She didn't want to go. She was happy here with the way things were. The thought of being a mother was just unappealing to her.

She glanced at him when he wasn't looking, studying all the little ways he had changed. He was taller by at least two inches and his face had lost some of its youth. The best change by far was that he had grown more serious and reserved.

She hoped they could start afresh and all their previous bickering could be put aside.

King Henry lavished his bastard son with further grants of lands and honours. Mary's own allowance was increased and she found she could suddenly afford to spend even more lavishly than before. Despite the hopes of all the old noble families and the Spanish ambassador, the former Princess Mary was not brought to court. She wasn't even forgiven by her father or let to wander in the garden. The king was pressing for the council to move against her or get her to sign the Act of Succession, declaring herself a bastard.

Mary was in her father's rooms. Her husband was playing chess with her brother, both men half listening to his rants.

"He should not waste any more time with her," her father swore. "She refuses to see sense."

"What would you have the king do?" her brother drawled. Mary watched from her seat as he moved a pawn forward, opening himself up to attack. He might lose his queen, but her husband was playing just as badly and didn't notice.

"If I had a daughter who was disobedient, I would make her see sense. If she continued to refuse, I would beat her until she didn't know up from down."

Mary jumped as his fists thumped on the table with

a loud bang. She fought to remain calm. Her father was just angry and speaking out of turn. Her brother noticed her discomfort and gave her a sympathetic look.

Their father went on. "I told the king as much in the council meeting this morning. But we will see if he acts upon it. All this dawdling makes him look weak. If he can't even control his own daughter."

"It is losing the Spanish alliance that he fears, not one little girl," Henry Fitzroy said with cold calculation.

Mary shivered, thinking of poor Mary Tudor. Did she know how these men spoke of her? Did she know it was not love that kept her father from striking her down for her disobedience?

"You are right," her father said with a grin. "We will make that Spanish ambassador apply the pressure himself. We must make him believe that the king is a second away from cutting down that imp."

Two weeks later Mary Tudor signed the act. Many rumours surrounded the event. Some said the pope had given her clemency in the form of a special license absolving her of all responsibility. She had signed under duress, so the solemn oath she had taken was void. In the future it could not be held against her.

Mary's husband tired of the excitement at court, retreated to St. James's Palace. After so many weeks of celebrations and outings, he had been feeling unwell. She was among the party that bade him farewell. Even as she kissed his cheek and promised to pray for his swift recovery, she knew she was happy to see him go.

Mary was getting ready for bed on her own. She craved a little privacy and silence. With that in mind she had sent Joyce and Agnes to sleep in their own adjoining room tonight. She was praying in front of her prie-dieu, something she didn't do as often as she should. Tomorrow would be another busy day, a joust followed by an archery tournament. She would wear a new green damask gown gifted to her by Jane Seymour. She appreciated the gesture, but more than a new gown she wished for a new headdress. With Jane's ascension the fashion had switched back to the gable hoods Katherine of Aragon preferred. There had been no time to have one properly fitted, so out of storage came her old hoods trimmed with gold and seed pearls.

She sighed, rubbing the side of her head where the hood had dug into her scalp. Her head was pounding. Then she realised the sound she heard was a soft tapping at her door. Curious, she tightened her heavy robe around her and cracked open the door. She was surprised to find Mary Shelton standing there, her eyes wide with excitement.

"Come, you must come," she whispered.

Without thinking, Mary let her pull her out of her bedchamber and they drifted through the palace, using secret passageways and staircases rarely used even by servants.

"Where are you dragging me off to?" She laughed.

Mary Shelton grinned. "You will see soon enough."

Arm in arm they turned the corner, padding down the hallway on soft slippers, not daring to breathe a word. It was then Mary noticed her cousin was clutching a Bible in her other hand. But they were nowhere near the chapel. These were bedchambers usually reserved for guests.

Mary Shelton stopped in front of a door. She glanced around the corridor, making sure no one was around before tapping on it. It was opened and a hand thrust a candle forward, illuminating their faces before they were allowed inside.

Mary paused on the threshold, not believing what she was seeing. There was Margaret Douglas, dressed in a magnificent gown and hand in hand with none other than her uncle, Thomas Howard the younger.

"What is this?" she said.

Margaret rushed forward, taking her hands in hers. "Mary, we are in love. We are to be married here and now. We want you to be one of the witnesses as we say our vows."

Mary took a step back in horror at her words. She looked at her uncle. He was avoiding her gaze.

"Uncle, this is madness."

Margaret dropped her hands. "I thought you'd be happy for us."

Mary cleared her throat. "Don't misunderstand me...I am just shocked. What will the king say? What will the duke?"

"We will wait for just the right moment. My uncle, the king, adores me. We will explain. He will understand," Margaret said.

"Why not ask for permission before this, then?" she asked, her eyes never leaving her uncle's face.

He turned to her at last with a wide smile on his lips. "We are determined to be happy. We cannot live apart any longer. If we tell them, they will argue against the match and find a way to separate us. This way they cannot."

"Why did you call me here?" she asked him. This was to put her in danger.

"You would never forsake us," he replied, a strange coolness to his tone. Mary gaped, but it all became clear. They must have thought about it and known that she alone would be fool enough to stand beside them when the fury of the council and king came down upon them. Any other might have denied ever seeing or hearing about this match. She remembered Sir Francis Bryan's warning. But she never thought matters had gone so far. Her uncle was a notorious flirt. Was he truly in love with Margaret?

Her eyes narrowed at him. So he was a Howard after all. Here was Margaret Douglas, a rich heiress and niece to the king, ripe for the picking. Who could resist such a grand match? Certainly not a Howard.

"Enough, Mary," her cousin said. "They are in love. How can we not support them?"

Mary looked at Mary Shelton and felt a deep pity for her. She was thinking of her own love, who died on the block. This was probably the first time in weeks she had seen her smile.

"Unless you run now to the king you are complicit in this," her uncle said into the ensuing silence. "So will you stand our witness?"

Mary's fingers, hidden in the folds of her gown, crossed themselves. "Very well, if you are intent on doing it anyway."

Margaret threw her arms around her neck and pulled her into a tight embrace. Mary was conflicted. She wanted nothing more than to push her away, but at the same time wasn't this what they all wished for? Love?

She watched as they said their vows, exchanged rings, and kissed. They enjoyed the wine and sweet-meats that had been secreted into the room by Mary Shelton. Then they stood guard as Margaret took her new husband into one of the adjoining rooms to enjoy the pleasures of the marriage bed.

Mary couldn't shake the feeling in the pit of her stomach that this was wrong. All wrong.

What madness possessed them? She was unable to sleep. Every little sound or creak had her leaping to her feet, listening at the door to the corridor. No one inter-rupted them. Mary Shelton teased her and then soon after midnight fell asleep in a large chair, her head leaning against the windowsill.

At the first signs of dawn, Mary couldn't take it anymore and woke them all. With one last kiss to his new wife, her uncle sprinted out of the room, leaving the two cousins to help his wife dress and look presentable.

"I need to get back to my rooms," Mary said as they finished lacing Margaret into her gown.

The women nodded. The adrenaline from the night before had waned, leaving them with the magnitude of what they had done.

"Mary, I am so happy you were here to witness us say our vows." Margaret was squeezing her hand.

"I am glad you are so happy. I wish you nothing but joy." She managed a smile for her friend. Perhaps they were right. It would all be well.

Over the next few days they all pretended nothing had happened. But Mary kept catching Margaret sneaking glances at her uncle and giggling when he noticed. They would find ways to be together, and once Mary had caught them coming up from the garden, Margaret's hood askew.

She flashed her uncle a glare on that occasion, but he merely grinned. Over time she relaxed. If it was a game to them, then she would treat it as such. She stopped trying to push them to confess what they had done to the king. After all, there never seemed to be a good moment.

They had a month of happiness.

Then it all unravelled around them. Mary wasn't sure how it happened. She had been with the queen's party, walking several paces behind, lost in her thoughts as she planned out which poem she should add to her brown book.

She caught the flash of skirts from the corner of her eye and saw Elizabeth Ughtred, the queen's sister, running past. She reached her sister and without preamble began to whisper in her ear some urgent news.

Jane remained composed and then silenced her sister with one look.

Up ahead the king was walking with his gentlemen. Mary thought she had seen Cromwell turn his head toward them.

They continued their walk, but when she could she sidled up to Lady Elizabeth and asked her what was wrong.

"I just saw something dreadful," she began but stopped herself. "It is not for me to comment on."

"Please tell me. I swear I won't repeat it," Mary said, suddenly desperate to know.

Lady Elizabeth looked at her with a knowing look. There were no secrets at court. But finally she relented.

"I just saw Margaret Douglas get taken away."

"Where?" Mary was incredulous.

"She's been arrested. She is being taken to the tower."

The world was spinning, and Mary didn't know how to make it stop. The edges of her vision were going black.

"Lady Elizabeth, help me."

When she awoke, Mary was in her bed. Agnes was sponging her forehead. She motioned for Mary not to say a word before turning to look behind her.

"She is awake, my lord."

The familiar shape of her father came into her line of sight. "You may leave us."

Mary wanted to ask Agnes to stay. She was terrified of the anger she could see in her father's eyes.

"Sit up," he said. "I assume you heard about that business my brother got himself messed up in. We shall hear everything now."

Mary struggled to sit up. Her head still felt light, but she dared not disobey him. She noticed there were two other men in the room. Thomas Cromwell was standing near the fireplace warming his hands, while a clerk had a pen in hand. His eyes met hers and she saw an eagerness in them that made her flinch.

She looked back at her father and knew that this going to be an interrogation. Mary shifted and winced as her head throbbed. She touched the side of her head to feel a bandage wrapped around it.

"You hit your head when you fainted. Silly girl," her father said. The hardness in his gaze didn't soften at her pain. Then he turned away from her. "Well, Cromwell, you may ask her what you like."

Mary stopped herself from calling out. Who could she call out for? Her own father was handing her off to the wolves.

He exchanged spots with Cromwell, who took a seat next to her bedside, hands clasped before him.

"Do not fret, Lady Mary. I am only here to talk and ask you a few questions about this business with the king's beloved niece and your uncle. Then you may rest and recover your strength, but it is imperative that you tell me everything you know."

She had heard of snake charmers before, whose steady gaze could mesmerise a viper into obeying their commands. She thought with a grimace she was in the presence of one. Any resolve she had to keep her mouth shut evaporated as the questions began. It seemed like they knew everything anyway.

When the men were gone and her ladies allowed to return, she fell back against her pillow and cried until she fell asleep. She woke the next day to the gentle prodding of Joyce.

"Your father wishes to see you, Your Grace." She spoke in hushed tones, as if Mary might still be ill.

"Very well," she said, her heart pounding faster by the minute. What could he want now? "I am feeling better. Don't worry about me."

"Yes, Your Grace," Joyce said, not believing her.

Mary allowed them to dress her in a russet

gown and plait her hair up before cramming the heavy hood on her tender head. She tried her best not to flinch. She led them out, her head held high, toward her father's rooms. He must have some plan to save his brother. All would be well. He would tell her what to do. This was all just a big mistake.

"Your things are being packed and you shall go to meet your husband at St. James's. You shall care for him."

Mary blinked, not understanding.

"He's still ailing, you foolish girl." Her father scoffed at her.

"Then he must call a doctor." She frowned.

"Did the fall make you an idiot?" He rolled his eyes. "Instead of being dragged into this, you shall be thankful to be sent from court to care for your ailing husband. We shall see what happens from there. But the king will be more sympathetic to you if you are by your husband's side."

Mary continued to stare dumbly at her father. "What about Uncle Thomas and Margaret? Where are they?"

He slammed his hand down on the arm of his chair and she flinched back. "In the tower. Where else would they be?"

"But they are in love. They married for love. You must help them. This would be a beneficial match for our family." She began rambling and looking anywhere but at her father, so she was taken unaware by the hard slap that stopped her mid-sentence.

Her hand touched her cheek that throbbed with pain.

"They are not married," he said. "Do you not see? The king has declared that my brother has seduced his niece and lain with her in sin. They are both in the tower."

Mary felt her own fury rise from some deep crevice within her as she stared at the man she had idolised her whole life. "You would kill your own brother?"

He surprised her by throwing his head back and letting out a loud barking laugh. He went on like this for quite some time. Finally, wiping the corners of his eyes with his sleeve, he regarded her with mirth. "It is not I who killed them. It is you."

She gripped her armchair tight. He was lying. What he said made no sense. She had spoken to no one about their wedding night. Had her maids noticed her absence?

Her father, still chuckling, walked over to his desk. He carried something in his hands. He tossed it down at her feet. Her heart skipped a beat at what she saw. Her book of poetry. Mary's eyes met her father's, a question on her lips.

He sneered at her. "We found this after, but we found a copy of several of your uncle's poems being passed around the court. They were really quite good," he said, half amused. "Too bad they spoke too clearly of his love for a certain lady. For a poet he certainly doesn't bother disguising much. But back to the point. Though they had been indiscreet, Cromwell wouldn't have had concrete proof without the poems you so diligently kept and circulated. It is you who put the final nail in their coffin, which is why you are being spared. I must congratulate you on your forethought."

"Then you will also know by now I was a witness to their union. My uncle didn't force himself on her or deflower her. They were married in the sight of God."

Her father laughed again. "No, you never saw such a thing because the king and Cromwell wish for you to never have seen such a thing. Do you understand?"

Mary got to her feet. "I will testify on their behalf." Her feelings of outrage and injustice squashed the fear she felt.

He laughed even harder. "Yes, do that. Put your head on the block as well. For that is where your actions will lead you. You should be on your knees, grateful that I am doing what I can to save you. Worthless as you are."

She folded within herself at his words. Her old desire to please him made her want to throw herself upon his mercy to ask what she could do to make him happy.

"Father, please. Is there nothing we can do for them? You cannot let your brother die. He is blameless."

"You can live. That is what you can do. You can let

nature take its course. The king's anger might abate with time. But if you go marching to him and tell him you were witness to his niece betraying him by marrying not only without permission but beneath her station, then he will never be able to forgive and forget the folly of two lovers." He softened as he spoke. "This is the only way. You will listen to me. I will not see you harmed by the folly they dragged you into. So go to your husband's side and tend to him in his hour of need."

The conversation was over. Mary was loath to admit that she was grateful for the inkling of kindness from him. At last she agreed. She could see no other way.

⚜

St. James's Palace was kept stifling hot. Her husband was indeed ill. The last time she had seen him he had grown tall and was showing signs of filling out into a figure similar to his father's, but now he looked more like a skeleton than a man. He had grown thin, and each cough made his whole body shake.

She was terrified of being in his presence for long. He had been surprised to find her by his side and sent her away more often than not.

"You don't know how to do it," he said, as if feeding him broth required years of training.

One day she tried to play the lute for him, but he

said her playing gave him a headache. It was not long before she gave up and simply kept out of his way. Sooner or later he would learn she had been sent here as punishment.

Her mind was battling with itself. Every time she dared to find hope for both her uncle and her friend, she would remind herself that she was a fool to trust the word of her father. She had seen the king do a lot worse over lesser offences. At least there was no further news. If the king was intent on killing them, he would have done so already.

Then late in July the doctors came to her rooms, pale and exhausted. They told her that there was nothing more they could do and that she should come to say goodbye to her husband.

She blinked, confused by what they were saying.

"Your husband might die," they said. "The king is sending his own doctors and physicians, but you should see him now while he is still lucid."

She nearly choked. Henry Fitzroy dying?

She went to his rooms, despite her fear of catching whatever was making him so sick.

He was propped up on pillows, his lips tinged blue and his skin sallow. She didn't want to get closer, but she forced herself to sit by his side and take his hand.

"My lord, is there anything I can do for you?" she said in such a small voice she had to repeat herself to make sure he heard.

He grunted by way of response but turned his face away from her. She took this to mean no.

"I can sit with you," she offered, but at that he managed to pull his hand away.

Mary looked to the doctors for help. They looked at each other sadly and motioned for her to come away.

"Don't fret, Lady Mary," one of them said. "He probably doesn't wish to cause you pain. Thank you for coming. We thought it might do him good."

Mary could see how desperate they were. If the king's heir died on their watch, what would the king do to them?

"I shall go pray for my husband's speedy recovery," she said, and hurried to the chapel with her ladies.

She remained kneeling before the crucifix for hours, rosary in hand, as she prayed in the old way. At first she prayed for Fitzroy—no one deserved such a terrible death—but then her mind turned to her uncle and Margaret. Who was praying for them? Who making sure that they didn't fall ill in the cold rooms of the tower? Her husband had a team of doctors and a large household looking after him, but they would have no one. She found she could no longer cry. Not even the immense guilt she felt drew tears from her eyes. She couldn't save them.

Slowly, even the feeling of guilt left her. She felt nothing. She was simply waiting. But waiting for what?

CHAPTER 9

Perhaps if she had known what would happen after she was widowed, she would have prayed harder for the health of her husband. Unfortunately, she didn't have the gift of foresight.

She returned to the queen's rooms dressed in dark navy, the other ladies eager to avoid her, left her to her own devices.

Her father was thankfully not here. He had gone to Norfolk to see to the burial of her husband. There wouldn't be a state funeral for him. The king had declared it was all to be done quietly and without any fuss.

Mary hadn't known how the king would react to the news, but she hadn't expected this. She recognised something of the emptiness in his eyes as she beheld him for the first time after he heard of his son's death. She guessed he was feeling just as betrayed and abandoned by God as she was. Too bad they couldn't have a tête-à-tête.

Mary waited for her husband's estate to be broken up. She would no longer have the rich allowance paid to her every quarter, but she was still entitled to a princely sum. She knew the lands that were to be her widow's jointure if her husband predeceased her. It had all been written out neatly in the marriage contract. But even after the house was disbanded and his wealth distributed, she received nothing.

She hoped her father would press the king, but she dared not ask him directly.

Then she wrote to the one person she never thought she would dare address directly— Cromwell. She asked to know why she wasn't given her widow's jointure. If there was some impediment.

The answer, when it came, was short and to the point but left her seething with rage.

The king has declared that you were not truly wed and are not entitled to your portion of his estate. He is allowing you to retain the gowns and jewels you purchased during your marriage.

Mary wanted to scream. So this was the punishment the king planned for her? She regretted feeling any sense of camaraderie with him. He was nothing but a bully.

If she was in her right mind she never would have picked up the pen to reply to Cromwell, but she wasn't entirely sane as she wrote, threatening that it was her legal right as Henry Fitzroy's wife. She laid out precedence, cited statutes and other laws. She said she wouldn't be afraid to bring this before parliament to have them debate the issue.

He wrote back that in a different life she would have made a good lawyer.

"You shall take your household and go to Kenninghall," her father said, standing beside his horse. "You aren't wanted in the queen's rooms. Some time away might do you good."

Mary bit her lower lip. She was being packed off, but this time it was without her own money or status beyond what being the widow of the king's bastard son might bestow on her, which was not much. This was especially true considering the king had never ordered the court to go into mourning. He was content to forget he ever had a son.

"I shall need time," she said, bargaining with her father.

"You shall leave next week," he declared. A hand reached up to steady his anxious horse. "You shall be grateful I am sending you there. I expect you to live quietly and contemplate all your failings."

"Yes, Father," she said gravely.

As she walked back to the queen's rooms, she thought anxiously of her uncle again. She wanted to see them one more time before she would be too far away to help. They had still not been released. Cromwell had passed a new law that said it was illegal for a relative of the king to marry without permission. The threat of treason hung over both of their heads. It might only be a matter of time before the axe fell.

She didn't know who to turn to for help. Finally, she approached Sir Francis Bryan, who looked at her reproachfully but as if he had expected she would seek him out sooner or later.

"There is nothing I can do to help them," he said. "I tried to warn you. I tried to warn him. Do not blame yourself."

"But I do," she whispered back. "I could have stood firm and told the world they were truly married."

He shook his head. "You would never have been allowed to speak. Put aside your guilt. Think of the future."

"I must see them again. Will you help me?" She dug her fingers into his forearm, not letting him pull away and make excuses. "Sir Francis can do anything. You travel the high seas and sneak into palaces, slitting the throats of your enemies. You seduce abbesses into dreadful sins. They call you the Vicar of Hell. Don't tell me you can't find some way for me to see my uncle and Margaret Douglas."

His eyes widened for a fraction of a second. Then he grinned. "She was a nun, not an abbess. Very well, my lady, I shall see what I can do."

She tried not to let her relief show. "I have less than a week."

He nodded. "I'll come find you. But remember it won't do them any good. Their case is hopeless."

"I don't care. It will be something," she said, making sure he could see how determined she was.

Her position at court fell even further as they commandeered her rooms for the queen's brother, Edward Seymour. Now she shared a room with two other ladies-in-waiting. They kept out of her way, so in the end she had more privacy than she normally would, as Joyce and Agnes were sent ahead to Kenninghall. She was sorry she had dragged them down with her. But they didn't ask to be released from her service either. Mary understood how it looked. Not only was she connected to Anne Boleyn, the first English queen to ever be executed, but she was now also widowed.

Rumours had stated that Anne had been trying to poison the bastard prince. Many looked Mary's way with suspicion. Hadn't she been by his side in the last days of his sickness? What if she had poured the last drop of poison down his throat? The king certainly wanted nothing to do with her. He was not kind or consoling. Mary wanted to shout that he was too busy forgetting Fitzroy ever existed, not that he thought she had murdered him. But what did that matter? In a way she was grateful to be leaving court. She kept feeling as though death stalked the royal apartments. Dead queens, heirs, and servants.

At supper that night a note was slipped into her hand.

Tomorrow at dawn, meet me at the stables.

She burned the note. She was sure that her father would hear of her visit sooner or later, but secrecy wasn't her goal. Mary merely wanted to see them before she could be stopped.

She tossed and turned all night before deciding she might as well go down to the stables. Mary pulled on her borrowed black cloak and made her way down. She found her horse saddled and ready for her. She petted the mare's velvet nose and fed her some oats.

"Glad you are punctual," Sir Francis Bryan said, stepping out from the shadows.

She glanced at him. He had not bothered to conceal his identity. Sir Francis wore an icy-blue silk suit and a daring cape to match. He would stand out like a beacon.

"Where do you find such ridiculous clothing?"

"You ought to be nicer to me," he huffed. "Are you ready?"

She nodded.

"Good. The faster we go, the faster you can come back," he said, holding out a hand to her. He lifted her onto her horse with practiced ease. Mary wondered how many ladies of the court he had secreted out in the early morning.

They rode through the palace gates without being stopped. Sir Francis Bryan merely tipped his hat to one of the guards and tossed him a coin.

He had taken to whistling as they made their way through the streets of London. It was still quiet and the noise he was making was jarring.

"Why didn't we take the barge upriver?" she asked, if only to stop him.

He looked at her with a half-smile. "I don't have any friends among the bargemen that would let us pass. Don't worry about it. I told you I'd take you to see them."

"You aren't worried about risking yourself?"

He shook his head. "I wouldn't be taking you if I was."

"Fair enough." Mary forced herself to focus on the road ahead.

By the time they arrived at the tower, bright sunlight had lit the streets.

He spoke to Kingston and then came back to fetch her. "Come along," he said.

It was so easy for him, but she supposed he was familiar with the tower and intimate with its workings. He led her through the tower first to Lady Margaret's rooms. He waited outside but told her she could not be long.

Margaret was being kept in a small room with only a closet off the main room. At least they furnished it sufficiently to keep away the cold and she had a proper mattress to sleep on.

Her friend was on her feet in an instant and ran to her, not even bothering with a hello before hugging her.

Mary thought she might be squeezed to death. "It's good to see you too," she said.

Margaret released her with a grin. "You've come. I knew you would. Oh, Mary, how did it come to this?"

Mary could have reminded her that she had tried to warn her, but what good would that do her? "I don't know," she said, unable to tell her friend the truth.

"We thought we took care, but clearly we didn't. Do you think the king will forgive us? Do you think he will allow me to see Thomas again? I cry night and day for him. We've been"—she leaned toward her to whisper— "exchanging letters."

"Oh, Margaret. But that could lead to more danger." Mary held her hand.

"What more harm can we do?" she said woefully. "My uncle, the king, seems content to let us rot in here, and we can do nothing but please him in this."

Mary let out a breath she was holding. "You can survive. His temper will cool—"

Margaret shook her head. "No, he will wish to forget about us. The only reason we haven't been put to death is that he fears his reputation if he were to sign our death warrants. But if we were to die in captivity then no one would blame him."

Mary gave her hand a comforting squeeze. "Don't think like that."

Tears were welling in Margaret's eyes. "But it's the truth. If only I had never met him. But love shook my heart, like the wind on the mountain, troubling the oak trees."

Mary couldn't help but smile. "You cannot be treated so cruelly if you can quote poems from antiquity to me."

"Sappho's work soothes me as I wilt away here in my cell." Margaret pulled away from her and went to the window. It was barely wide enough for her to stick her head through. Nothing more. "Sometimes they let me go for a walk outside on the turrets, but how much longer can I be here? Perhaps you can ask the king? You can tell him that Thomas and I are truly married. He didn't seduce me into his bed."

Mary held up her hand to stop her. "This is his doing. He knows but doesn't care. It suits him to think you were seduced and not truly married. He had great plans to marry you off, and he cannot do that anymore."

Margaret scoffed. Clearly, despite her confinement, she didn't understand the gravity of her situation.

"My husband is dead. The king ignores me and pretends I don't exist. I don't have my widow's jointure and my father won't fight for my rights. I am penniless, as my great dowry has reverted to the king.

Margaret, I cannot help you," Mary said swiftly. "I am sorry."

When Margaret looked at her again, she could see she was about to cry.

"How can I live without him?"

Me, me, me. That was all Mary heard. She pitied her friend, she truly did, but she wasn't comprehending the situation she now found herself in all because of her actions. Perhaps it would have been kinder to have been arrested as well.

"All you can do is survive and make sure your love never gets forgotten."

A thought struck Margaret then. She went over to the rough writing desk in the far corner of the room and pulled out a few sheets of paper.

"Keep these for us then, in case..." She struggled to finish her thought. "...something was to happen to us. It's just a few love letters. Silly things, but you might find some of them worthy of being in that book of yours."

"I-I don't think I can ever pick up the pen again," Mary said. "Look at the trouble it's got us in."

Margaret shook her head. "No, you cannot throw it aside. Promise me."

"Very well," Mary said, unable to find the strength to refuse her.

"Poetry has always been a refuge for the both of us. Not just a silly pastime. We would have been found out one way or another," Margaret said, sniffing as she tried to hold back her tears. "As you said, we were foolish to marry without the king's permission. Nothing but a foolish pair of doves in love."

A tap at the door.

"I must go, and I don't know when or if I can ever come back," Mary said. "I will hold on to these poems for you though. Take care."

The two women hugged before Sir Francis opened the door and motioned for her to come along.

"If you see him, tell him I regret nothing," Margaret called out after her.

Mary tucked the papers away, hoping they would survive the journey back to court. If Sir Francis saw, he said nothing and on he went.

Her uncle was kept in the opposite wing, as far away as possible from Margaret.

His cell was bare. Unlike Margaret, who still had tapestries and other small luxuries, they kept him in a much worse state. Mary had noticed even Sir Francis Bryan's smile falter for a moment.

"I am surprised you came," he said, not bothering to get up.

Mary was hurt. "Of course I did. I have seen Margaret as well. She sends you her love and devotion. She wouldn't turn back time and undo anything."

He nodded, his expression pensive. "Do you have any news from the court? Is there any sign we might be released or that my brother will speak for me?"

Mary turned her head so he would not see the

anguish in her eyes. "You need something on the walls to help keep the drafts out. Maybe stoke a bigger fire," she commented.

"Yes, it's very easy to put in a request with Kingston. I can't believe I have neglected that until now." Then he laughed at his own sarcasm.

"I am sorry, Uncle. I am sorry I cannot do more for you. If I could I would bribe and cajole the guards, but I am penniless." She took off a small ruby ring. "Take this. Perhaps it can buy you a few more blankets."

His expression softened. "I am sorry to have dragged you into this. I was not a good uncle to you."

"We are practically the same age." She waved him off. "I could've gone running to the king. But tell me something. Tell me you truly loved her and you weren't just making a play for ambition's sake. I swear on my life I will never tell."

His lips pursed, insulted by her line of questioning. "Is that why you came all this way? Would you even believe my answer?"

"I would."

"Then I will say this. I love her truly. There was some calculation behind my decision to go through with the ceremony. To take the risk. I would not let myself become completely besotted by love for a milk-maid, but it doesn't change the fact that I do love Margaret and I have staked my life on it."

"The king might forgive you." The words felt

empty as they left her mouth. They hung over them, a blanket of false hope.

He shook his head. "He might forgive her, and I pray every night he does, but I will never be free again. And if they were to release me, I would still not be free. They would send me away and I would never see her again."

She reached out to him, but he pulled away.

"Go now, before you drive me into further misery. I am sorry for your part in this. You could have had a clean conscience, but I selfishly dragged you into danger."

"There are worse punishments than being sent back to Kenninghall."

"You must take care of yourself. Your father doesn't forgive easily, either. Why do you think he doesn't fight for you to have your fortune? He will try to tear you down. Don't let him make you into his puppet."

Mary clenched her fists. "That I can promise you."

She left him to his thoughts, praying he would find a way to be optimistic again. But nothing about the tower lent itself to hope.

On the way back to the palace she wept for herself and for them. She had never realised what feeling helpless had truly felt like until now.

Sir Francis Bryan helped her from her horse, handing the reins to a waiting groom. He patted her back in slow rhythmic motions.

Something about the strange motion drew a laugh

from her lips. "You are patting me as if I were your horse. How did you ever seduce anyone into your bed?"

He choked on a laugh.

"Lady Mary, I do not know. It must be my devilish good looks." He winked at her with his one good eye. Then his expression turned serious. "I am sorry. I tried to warn you it would only make you feel worse to see them."

She managed a smile. "No, that's where you are wrong. So thank you for taking me."

Mary Shelton pulled her aside on her last day at court.

"I am sorry to see you go," she said. "I hope you will be back soon."

"I don't think I will," Mary said truthfully. There was no point hoping for something that might never come. If by some good fortune she was summoned back, it wouldn't be on her own terms. She would have to do her father's bidding. After all, without him she would be destitute. From now on she would be living on his charity.

"I wish I could go with you," Mary Shelton whispered. "There's nothing at court for me anymore."

Mary pulled her cousin into a tight embrace. "You will heal. It won't make you forget him, but it will hurt less. Perhaps someday you will only remember the happiness you shared together. He wouldn't want you to be wasting away."

Mary Shelton nodded. "Thank you for believing I loved him."

"Of course." She looked at her, a question forming on her lips.

"Everyone looks at me and thinks I have no feeling. I am a great silly whore. Renowned around the court for being light with my favours. I can't understand why that makes me incapable of love?" She was halfway to sobbing again.

Mary could only shake her head. "They don't know. They are all fools."

Her cousin laughed between tears. "All of them?"

"Yes."

"Write to me often. I will write to you. I promise I won't forget this time," Mary Shelton said.

They shared one last embrace and then Mary was left alone once more to her own devices. She returned to her room. In the doorway, she looked around her. There was a roomful of memories to store away.

She was packed off to Kenninghall without so much as a farewell. When she arrived after weeks on the road, she found herself completely deflated. She moved through the motions of rising early, eating, praying, riding out like she always did, but she didn't feel like herself and after a time she kept to her rooms more and more.

She felt forgotten both by her friends at court and her own family. Mary was here under her own version of house arrest. She thought of her mother for the first time in years. Was this what it was like for her too? She shuddered. No wonder she had become so bitter.

Then one day, Mary was surprised to find herself joined one morning by none other than her father's mistress. Lady Bess was nearing her mid-thirties but was still a striking woman with golden hair and striking green eyes.

She stood before her, waiting to be invited to sit.

"What can I do for you, Lady Bess?" she asked.

"I've come to ask you if you wished to help me plan out a new garden. I am on a strict budget and I find I cannot focus on numbers right now."

Mary blinked. That was the last thing she expected to hear. But the prospect of a task appealed to her.

"I would be happy to help."

"Very well, I shall see you in my rooms after dinner," she said with a brilliant smile that illuminated her face.

Life became more tolerable after that. Her father's mistress kept her busy with all sorts of projects and household tasks. She helped keep an inventory of the buttery, the stores of food. She rode out to inspect the tenant farms and reported back to Lady Bess, who would ensure workmen were hired to repair leaky roofs or cracked walls.

She began flourishing once more.

"Why have you taken me under your wing?" she asked Lady Bess one day. "I was quite rude to you before."

Lady Bess chuckled. "Would you believe me if I said you weren't the first, nor were you the rudest? You are also not the only one stuck here twiddling her thumbs. I found I could tolerate it better if I kept busy and my mind off the fact I have nowhere else to go."

Mary tilted her head to the side, confused. Where would she want to go but here?

Lady Bess, guessing her thoughts, gave her a woeful smile. "When your father first looked my way and offered to give me a place, I gave up a normal life. No one would have me now. My family doesn't approve of me. I have nieces and nephews I have never met. I represent nothing but shame to them. So, without realising it, I became stuck here. Everything I have can disappear in an instant. I'm sure you know what that is like."

Mary felt a lump in her throat. "Yes, I know." She couldn't bear to see the sorrow and pity directed at her.

Mary was grateful to be pulled into a world of accounts and projects around the estate. She wrote consistently to Mary Shelton, who did her best to keep her up to date with all the gossip she could want. It was how she heard that Jane Seymour was expecting her first child. From then on, every day she went to the chapel to pray for her health and the health of the baby she carried. Mary hoped that if Jane gave him a son then the king might be in a forgiving mood. Her uncle and Margaret Douglas were still under arrest in the tower. They could be released.

All she could offer them were prayers.

The allowance she was given was a pittance. The king had been moved by pity to allow her the sum of fifty pounds annually from his son's estates. With all her other expenses, she barely had enough to buy wood for the winter months. Her father was not forthcoming with any further grants of money. He was intent on seeing her humbled to dust. Just as stubbornly, she refused to beg him for more money. She stayed huddled in her rooms underneath her furs and robes or kept to the great hall where the fires were always built up high.

Then, in summer, as she was watching them lay new tile in the dairy, she spotted a small retinue coming up the road. Mary saw the banners of her brother flying. She looked down at herself. She must look like a mess. Her hair was tied back in a simple white cap and her gown was old and dusty. Where had the fashionable duchess gone?

She set aside the apron she was wearing and made

her way to the main house. Her brother looked at her in mild surprise.

"You look like you could use a bath," he tried to say, but then his face fell. "May I speak to you alone?"

Henry was not acting like himself. She knew he must have come with bad news and steeled herself against disappointment.

They were in an empty office, one that the steward used each quarter to hand out the wages to the staff. She turned and waited for him to speak.

"Sit down, Mary," he said, his tone soft and pleading. "I have some terrible news."

She didn't move. "Just tell me, Henry."

He let out a long sigh. "Our uncle has died. He was ill this past winter, and this summer he worsened. He is gone."

Tears clouded her vision, but she forced herself to remain on her feet. "And Margaret?"

"She was moved to Syon Abbey. The king has still not forgiven her."

She nodded. "At least she is safer out of the tower. From sickness and disease, I mean. I have prayed for her. Prayed for them both."

"I know."

She was angry at that. Angry at the sadness and pity in his voice. "How could you know what it is to lose a friend?"

"He was my uncle too, and he is not the first I have lost over the years. I have never seen you shed a tear for your husband, but I have, for he was my dearest friend," he said, an angry, familiar snap to his words.

Mary looked away from him.

"I wanted to come here to tell you in person. Father doesn't seem to care much. I don't think he would have even written to tell you," he said.

Mary listened to him as he railed on and complained about their father. How he never took him seriously and how he never gave him the respect he deserved. She would have pitied him more if he was not a man with lands and a title in his own right. He was not at the mercy of their father.

"Anyway, I came to give you something else." He looked sullen and shy as he handed her a folded piece of paper.

"What is this?" She was genuinely surprised to unfold it to find a poem scratched out in his hand.

"I wrote it," he said, as if he was confessing a dreadful sin. "I think it belongs in that book of yours. You will recognise the subject."

She was caught off guard by the beautiful words. "You wrote this? I had no idea you were interested in poetry."

The corners of his lips twitched. "There's much we don't know about each other. I believe you have some of my work copied out in your book. Father let me see it," he added as explanation.

"Ah." Mary was utterly at a loss.

"I cannot stay long. Father has summoned me back to London." He left her there in the darkened room.

In another life they might have been friends. She felt the urge to call out to him to ask him to take her with him. She stared back down at the words on the page, finding it hard to imagine that Henry Howard, Earl of Surrey, could write such verse:

> For you yourself do know, it is not
>   long ago
> Since that for love one of the race did
>   end his life in woe,
> In tower both strong and high, for his
>   assured truth,
> Whereas in tears he spent his breath,
>   alas, the more the pity!
> This gentle beast so died, whom
>   nothing could remove,
> But willingly to seek his death for loss
>   of his true love.

CHAPTER 10

Mary found herself celebrating yet another Easter at Kenninghall. Between working on her poetry and the estate two years had passed her by.

She had grown accustomed to life in the country. Living in half disgrace had taught her humility, but she still found escape in her literary pursuits. Thomas Wyatt occasionally remembered to send her his newer poems and Mary Shelton became a reliable correspondent, keeping her abreast of court gossip.

When Mary read her latest letter saying that the king was intent on marrying again, she suspected her time at Kenninghall was coming to an end.

Her father would never let an asset sit unused for long. A new queen was arriving soon from faraway Germany, and her father had contrived it so most of the ladies of her household were Howards. Mary wondered if he was hoping for another of them to catch the king's attention. She didn't worry too much. She was grateful for the change in scenery and to be reunited with Margaret Douglas once more.

They had both changed in their time apart. Margaret's face was no longer that of a young ingenue. There was a seriousness in her gaze that was never there before. She was a woman who had tasted sorrow.

For her part, Mary felt unsure in her own skin, more like an old dame than a young woman of twenty-one. Her father had given her three new gowns for her return to London. Everything else she owned was old-fashioned and unsuitable for this new court.

Mary Shelton was there too, eager to tell them all the news. She had been there among the ladies that served Queen Jane in her last days. An infection following the birth of her son had taken her life. The king had been distraught for weeks following her death. Many had feared for the king's life, but here he was preparing to embark on his fourth marriage to another Anne.

By now all of England knew not to get attached to a queen. They were becoming interchangeable year by year.

When Mary first laid eyes on Anne of Cleves, in her unfashionable dress and with her stilted speech, she knew the poor woman would not sit on her throne for long.

The queen's attendants were all pretty and well-trained young ladies chosen from among the great noble families. Her father had paid a large sum in bribes to have so many Howard girls added to the roster. One in particular turned heads wherever she went. Her name was Kitty Howard, and she was far sillier than Mary Shelton had ever been. Not that anyone seemed to mind or criticise her for it. They were dazzled by her vivacious spirit and beauty. The king couldn't keep his eyes off her.

The royal marriage got off to a rough start, and the king was already speaking about how displeased he was with Anne of Cleves. Despite her initial fumbling, she was making a genuine effort to learn English. She even abandoned her German clothes in favour of English fashions. The common people loved her, but that didn't matter.

It was June when her father summoned her into his rooms for a private interview. Her brother, Kitty Howard, and Jane Rochford were there already.

She bowed and kept her eyes downcast.

"Sit," he commanded, and she obeyed without a second thought. He cleared his throat and addressed the party.

"The king is looking to break off the marriage to the Cleves woman," he said without preamble.

Mary could have choked. She looked from one to another of the other people assembled there. Only her brother was surprised by the announcement.

"He no longer needs an alliance with the duke, so"—her father clapped his hands together— "we must find a clean way for him to put the marriage aside."

"But they were married," Kitty Howard said, in that lyrical voice of hers. "We all saw it."

Mary saw her father's exasperated expression, but he tempered his disapproval with a smile. "And that brings me to my next point. I assume the three of you ladies can confirm the queen is still a maid?"

Mary could see Jane Rochford had remained impassive but leaned forward in her seat, eager to be called upon. "As far as I have been told."

Mary nodded, but it was Kitty Howard who laughed, not realising the seriousness of what they were discussing. "He doesn't touch her. She repulses him. We all find her in the morning as we left her at night. Her bedsheets are barely rumpled."

"What would you know about rumpled bedsheets, Lady Katherine?" her father asked the girl, who looked away meek as a kitten.

"Nothing, of course," she said.

"But that is good. The marriage can simply be annulled if it was never properly consummated. It would be the work of a day." He leaned back in his chair, smiling before turning to Kitty Howard. "The king has expressed that he wishes you to leave court."

"What? But why? What have I done?"

"Quiet," he said. Kitty balked but obeyed. Mary could see how exasperated her father was getting with Kitty. Why should he be surprised? She wasn't known for being intelligent. "The king admires you. He dotes on you. He might wish to make you queen."

"Me?" Kitty's voice came out like a squeak.

"Yes." He nodded.

Mary shared a look with her brother, who arched an eyebrow in wonderment. Kitty Howard was not the sort of girl you married and made queen. She was more the sort that would invite you to her bed on a whim.

"So we must safeguard your reputation. You must not be at court while the king is busy divorcing the current queen."

"Won't he forget about me?" she asked. The first genuine question to be asked.

"No." Her father started speaking slowly. "You will still be in London. I daresay he will wish to visit you. Bishop Gardiner has offered to house you."

Mary knew then that this was not simply the king's desire but a plot hatched up by the Catholic lords wishing to return England to Rome. A Howard girl in his bed who was raised in the old ways and controllable was the ideal queen for them. She might convince King Henry to turn away from his reformations.

"From now on you will all report to me who the queen sees and what she does. We need evidence, especially if she is trying to make a run for it."

"Where would she go?" Mary spoke at last. Her gaze fixed on her father. "Where could she go?"

He shrugged. "Just in case. Besides, an escape attempt looks just as guilty."

Mary nodded and resumed staring at her lap. Anne of Cleves would be right to flee. The king had no qualms about sentencing women to death.

Currently, the Countess of Salisbury was in the tower, an old woman who had been a friend to the king's mother, with royal blood in her veins. Anne Boleyn had been the love of the king's life, the woman he had waited six years for, and he had still called for a French headsman to behead her. So anything was in the realm of possibility with this king.

On their way out of the room, her brother followed on her heels.

"Mary, wait," he said, a hand to her elbow.

She let him lead her away to an open window.

"You truly think Kitty Howard would make a good queen?" he asked her in hushed undertones.

"No," she said, shaking her head. "But it is clear this is what father wants, and I will not stand in his way."

He seemed incredulous. "She is pretty, I give her that. But he would tire of her."

"Maybe, or maybe not. But what the king wants, he gets. Much like our father. I don't know if he wishes to have someone as tempestuous as Anne Boleyn by his side again."

At last her brother shrugged. "Well, I hope he doesn't blame me for this. There were other better options to throw in the king's way."

She gave him a look inviting him to tell her, but he merely smiled and patted her arm. "Take care."

She was glad she hadn't placed any bets with her brother on who would be queen and for how long. Anne of Cleves had given the king the divorce he wanted without putting up a fight. She had been rewarded by being granted a great fortune. The blame for the disastrous marriage fell upon Cromwell's shoulders alone. Her father had outmanoeuvred him for once, and he was executed outside the tower.

The king was happy with Kitty Howard for over a year. She might have barely been able to sign her own name, but she was a consummate actor. She excelled at playing the part of a madly in love woman, and the king lapped it up, believing her declarations.

When it was discovered that she had been sneaking lovers into her rooms after the king had fallen asleep, she was promptly arrested and questioned before being sent to the tower.

This time the queen's guilt was clear. They didn't have to invent evidence or torture confessions out of people. They found letters she wrote to Thomas Culpeper in her room in a messy scrawl that could only be her own. Worst of all, she even confessed to her sins.

Mary pitied her. She didn't even have the wit to

deny the accusations. Nor could she understand why she was being charged with treason as though she thought it was normal for a wife to have lovers. What could be said for her was that she had died bravely.

The days before the execution had been dark days for the Howards. They were all under suspicion. But Mary trusted that her father would find a scapegoat.

In the end it came down to a few words written in black ink. Her father laid out everything for the king in a neat, even hand. He explained that this was all his stepmother's fault. The Dowager Duchess of Norfolk had been lax in her upbringing of Kitty and concealed her true nature from everyone, including himself.

The king listened to him. Perhaps it was Gardiner whispering in his ear that made him accept her father's explanations. Or perhaps it was the fact that her brother, the Earl of Surrey, had become a great favourite with the king. It didn't matter. What mattered was that they were safe. Even the dowager duchess died before the king could decide if he should have her executed for her crimes.

After this Mary thought the king might be shaken and decide to live out the remainder of his days as a single man. He had reinstated both Princess Mary and Lady Elizabeth back into the line of succession. Prince Edward was growing strong in the nursery, becoming more like his father day by day. There were plenty of other heirs as well. The king didn't need to embark on another marriage.

However, Mary soon discovered he was undeterred by his past experiences. The hunt for a sixth wife had begun.

She was attending a family dinner, and her brother and father were discussing who the king might choose.

"Why not Mary?" her brother said.

Which prompted her to go into a coughing spree to hide her gasp of disgust. Mary was sure her brother was joking. If the king had set aside his brother's widow, how could he take up with the widow of his son? Besides, she saw what happened to his queens. She was not about to put her head on the block. No amount of glory and riches could compel her.

Her father shook his head. "No, I don't think he's ready for another Howard girl. We are lucky we came out of that alive."

"They say he likes Lady Catherine Latimer, but we will see what comes of it. Her husband is still alive," her father said after giving it some thought.

"The king might help him to his grave," her brother joked.

"You may not speak like that." Her father's eyes flashed with anger. "He could turn back to Anne of Cleves, but I doubt he will."

❧

The widowed Lady Catherine Latimer arrived at court as a lady-in-waiting in Princess Mary's household.

Catherine was everything that Kitty Howard was not. She was calm, composed and educated. She carried herself with a regal bearing that caught the king's eye.

It was only a matter of time before the king proposed. Mary wondered why she didn't run away while she could. Perhaps she had no other option.

Mary herself had no say in where she went or what she did. To maintain her estate she had pawned off her jewels and nicer clothes long ago. She was completely at her father's mercy, and though it didn't sit well with her, there was absolutely nothing she could do about it. That wasn't even the worst of it. The worst part was that he knew.

Mary had always seen him as a kind father who guided her with a firm hand, but now she saw him as a tyrant who might choose to dispose of her whenever he tired of her.

In the evenings, she dreamt of escape and during the days prayed for release.

৩৵৩

The king married Catherine Latimer in July. Like all his previous weddings it was small and private. There was no pretence that she would be crowned alongside him. By now everyone knew Henry wouldn't crown his queens unless they had given him a son.

Mary entered her service with a weary smile. This

would be the sixth queen she had served, and she wondered if she would be the last.

Margaret Douglas was by her side, as confused by the turn of events these last few years as she was.

They kept to themselves, writing poetry and sharing it between themselves. Neither of them felt inclined to start circulating their work or talking to others about their love of poetry. They had seen first-hand what trouble that could bring.

It was her brother Henry that took up the mantle of court poet. The Earl of Surrey was loud and boastful of his talents. Mary still believed that, despite his skill, he couldn't hold a candle to Thomas Wyatt's work. Too bad Wyatt wasn't at court to compete with him.

After he had been released from the tower he kept falling in and out of favour with the king and was rarely at court. She had seen him a handful of times over the last few years and never for long. Then the tragic news of his death reached them. He died at his home in Dorset after a prolonged illness he caught from his last diplomatic mission overseas. She couldn't believe he had died, but she was grateful more than ever for the poetry he had left behind.

That manuscript she had printed of his works was circulated but fell out of print as often as he fell out of favour with the king. Maybe now with his death it would be treasured. His words deserved to be read by future generations.

"You are lost in your thoughts," Margaret said softly.

Mary blinked to clear her mind. "I feel as though I have lived a hundred lifetimes. I feel tired. A tiredness in my very soul."

"You've been reading too much poetry," Margaret said with a laugh.

Mary shook her head, returning to her embroidery. A field of Tudor roses done in gold thread on the queen's sleeves. It was only half finished but already looked beautiful.

Years ago Mary owned hundreds of sleeves such as these. Now she had to go begging. Everyone still referred to her as "Your Grace" and "Duchess," but she was the poorest duchess she had ever heard of. Perhaps that would be how she could go down in history. The thought brought a smile to her face.

Catherine Parr's court was lively with learning and debate. She loved the reformed faith and invited scholars from universities to come lecture in her rooms.

A new door was opened for Mary as she gingerly stepped into this new world, anxious as a newborn.

Catherine invited her to speak and share her opinions. Sometimes the topics leaned toward the heretical. The thought of women preaching the word of God was absurd, but they listened to a holy woman preach anyway. They were invited to translate parts of the Bible from Latin into English, an exercise that presented a new challenge to her. She was enjoying herself immensely.

When Charles Blount came to lecture them on the civil obedience a subject owed a king, she was amazed to find he had become such a renowned scholar. He was no longer a boy doing the bidding of other men. He had become a man, teaching at Cambridge and writing essays that were published all over Europe.

She couldn't believe this was a man she had once dared kiss.

If he remembered, he never let on.

At night she dreamed of a life that could have been if they were both free to marry. She imagined she would have been happy.

In the morning she made herself forget this forbidden dream. There had never been love between them. What had she felt but desire? It was better he remained as he was, untainted by court politics and its machinations. He had always drifted among them without ever truly becoming a courtier.

In the winter of 1544, the king announced his intentions to declare war on France. This had been a desire he had held for years, but the kingdom's finances had never been good enough to sustain a war until now.

The council could not argue with him. They all feared the alliance between the Scots and the French.

King Henry had attempted to arrange a betrothal between the infant Queen Mary and his son Prince Edward. This offer had been refused, and she had quickly been betrothed to the French dauphin. The war against the Scots was going well. Now was the time to press their advantage.

Mary's father was honoured by being named commander of one of two armies that the king would take into France. Mary was grateful she would escape the yoke of his gaze for at least a few months.

There was another piece of news that left her feeling more alone than ever.

Margaret Douglas came to her one morning, tears brimming in her eyes.

"Mary, I am to be married," she said, unable to keep the news or excitement hidden from her for long.

Mary gaped. "What?" After all these years the king had found her a husband? Mary couldn't believe it. She was surprised by the tug of envy she felt welling in the pit of her stomach. She forced herself to smile.

"To who?"

"His name is Matthew Stewart, Earl of Lennox. He is very handsome," she said with a childlike giggle Mary hadn't heard in years.

"You are already halfway in love with him, I see. I am happy for you. Truly I am."

Margaret took her hand in hers. "You will find happiness too. Your father is bound to make a match for you sooner or later. He won't let you wither away."

Mary nodded, but she didn't think her father would care.

The wedding between Margaret and Matthew marked the beginning of the French campaign, and the rest of winter and much of the spring was spent gathering supplies, provisions, and weapons. Ships were armed with guns and plans were drawn up. In the queen's rooms, banners were being sewn with a speed never before seen.

By June the English army was ready to depart.

The king honoured Catherine Parr by naming her regent to rule in the name of his son Edward. It was a sweet scene to see the little prince trying to stand tall before his father as he was invested with the power to govern England.

Mary watched in amazement as Catherine Parr didn't balk at the great power bestowed upon her. She ruled with an even head, ordering both men and provisions to be sent to the king's armies with the ease a country wife might send the harvest to market.

But Catherine Parr's enemies were watching. They weren't pleased to see how she thrived and promoted the reformed faith.

Mary thought there was nothing they could do to her. Catherine Parr was an untouchable force of power and will. God surely smiled on her, and the king loved her.

The king returned victorious from France having captured Boulogne and signed a peace treaty with the exhausted King Charles of France. But a dark cloud had followed him home.

The gears of his suspicious mind had begun churning.

Mary stared at the trunks of new clothes being brought into her father's presence chamber.

Her father and brother were standing, inspecting the gowns inside. Every once in a while they would comment on one or another of them.

"I think she would look good in the silver," her brother said with a backward glance to her. "It would contrast nicely with her dark hair."

Her father grunted. "It will have to do."

"What is going on?" she asked at last, as the last of her patience wore thin.

Thomas Howard looked at his son and motioned for him to speak to her.

Mary let her brother pull her away from the prying eyes and ears of the servants.

"Father is intent on making a great match for you. But first we must see if you can catch his interest." He spoke in a hurried whisper. A wild hunger was in his eyes as he regarded her.

Mary felt the urge to step away from him.

"A marriage? Not Thomas Seymour again?" A year ago her father had attempted to see if he had been interested, but he would not take her without a large dowry. That was something her father was unwilling to supply. Mary had been grateful that plan had fallen through, but maybe it was to be revived again.

"No, not Seymour. We think you can reach higher." His eyes were twinkling mischievously.

Mary found her mouth was dry. "Tell me, Henry. What do you and Father have planned?"

He grinned, leaning forward to whisper in her ear. "The king. We have the king within our sights again. He is displeased with the queen. Gardiner is questioning some of her ladies as we speak..."

"No," she mouthed, but he did not hear her and continued.

"He shall put the heretic queen aside, and then you will step into her place."

"No," she repeated, but still he pressed on.

"You will give him a son and then you will be crowned queen. One day a Howard will sit on the throne."

"No," she said, loud enough so he couldn't ignore her. "What you are saying is..." She shook her head, horrified. "I will not hear of it."

He took hold of her arm, his expression of utter joy melting away. "Stop it, Mary. Think for a moment about the family and the heights we could rise to. You are pretty enough. You can do it."

"No," she repeated over and over again until he released her.

"You are overcome with the honour Father is arranging for you," he said, stepping away from her. "You will come to see that this is for the best. Mary, you will be obedient." His head cocked to the side, considering her. "You've always done as you are told."

Mary fled her father's rooms and ran to the queen's chapel, kneeling before the altar.

Her father and brother had run mad. She would throw herself from the parapets rather than allow them to push her into the king's marriage bed.

Her tears turned to rage at the impossibility of her position. She was thankful no one was nearby to hear her as she began pounding her fists into the stone tile until blood poured from her knuckles. *No. No. No.*

She was pleased to note that her father had miscalculated. He had underestimated Catherine Parr and her tenacity to stay alive.

It had been a very close thing.

The queen discovered that her enemies, Gardiner and the lord chancellor, were moving against her. A stream of arrests and accusations of heresy against those reformers who she supported alerted her to her danger. She devised the perfect plot and rushed to the king's side to placate any suspicions he might have. No one knew what she said, but it worked.

The next day, when the lord chancellor arrived to

arrest her with a troop of guards, she was walking arm in arm with the king. Upon seeing them she swayed, her eyes fluttering as though she was about to faint in his arms. The king held her steady and began publicly berating the lord chancellor, who fled the scene.

Now it was the supporters of the old faith that were on the run as the tide turned in favour of the reformers who supported Queen Catherine.

Mary had been hiding from her father for the whole duration of this ordeal, and when it was over and Catherine Parr was still at the king's side she saw her way to freedom.

Her father would never cease to move her about the board, a pawn in his play for power, and she didn't want to risk being sacrificed any longer.

She squared her shoulders and walked to Bishop Cranmer's rooms, ready to tell her tale.

Mary shivered despite the stifling heat of the room. The magnitude of what she was doing hit her. She supposed her reaction was natural. Who wouldn't be sick with anxiety while betraying their family?

"Are you certain you wish for me to go to the king with this tale?" Cranmer said, clearing his throat.

They had been closeted together for the good part of an hour. He had been surprised but attentive to her when she appeared at his apartment, demanding to speak to him. Perhaps he thought she was here to beg for money. Certainly, he hadn't been expecting her to tell him that her father was plotting treason.

She leaned forward. "You wouldn't be a dutiful servant to the king if you didn't report what I said."

A thin smile spread across his face. "You are right, Lady Mary, but I want you to be very certain that you have the stomach for what might come next. If we discover your father has been plotting against the king as a witness, your testimony will be required. Can you bring yourself to stand against him so publicly?"

Her body was rebelling against her. The chill crept into her bones as her anxiety grew greater with each second that passed. Mary took in a deep steadying breath, held it for as long as she could before releasing it.

"I have no choice. I am loyal to the crown above all else." It was a courtier's answer, but she didn't think it would be necessary to point out to him that her family had no qualms about using her as a tool in their plots without a care for her safety.

"That is commendable of you, my dear lady. I applaud your bravery. Your father is a great man, but I feel he has never taken care of you as he ought. Not that I should criticise a great duke of the realm."

They sat in silence as Cranmer finished making a few notes. Mary had become fixated by a tapestry depicting the Garden of Eden. "It's not bravery. It's about survival."

Life continued on as normal, the country began preparing for yet another Christmas. No one suspected Cranmer was sniffing out treason and corruption on behalf of the king. The court had just returned from a lovely excursion out on the Thames when a troop of Yeomen of the Guard approached the royal party. From afar Mary saw them arrest her brother, Henry, Earl of Surrey.

She watched him being dragged off red with fury. Mary was sure they were taking him away for questioning, nothing more. Cranmer was after her father, not him. She imagined that elsewhere in the palace the yeomen were barging into her father's apartments to arrest him as well.

But as it turned out, her father and brother were involved in more than just plotting to make her queen. They were aiming far higher. Her brother even had documents drawn up to prove the Howards were entitled to the throne of England. It hadn't taken much digging on Cranmer's part to uncover this plot. Her brother's tendency to boast had been his undoing. Mary shouldn't have been surprised to discover that he was a man without scruples. He would have been happy to drag her down with him. So she pitied him but she wouldn't lift a finger to help him.

Her father's castles and great houses were all searched. The evidence of treason was piling up against him. He attempted to plead with the king to spare his life. In fear, he blamed everything on his son's ambitions. Thomas Howard screamed in his cell that he was innocent. He should be spared.

At her father's trial, Mary walked in with her head held high to testify against him. In the antechamber, her mother and Lady Bess were waiting their turn. The women the Duke of Norfolk had always treated as his chattel would be the ones who brought him down. She found this intoxicating.

Mary approached the dais, her gaze unwavering even as her father turned to stare at her. She had never seen such fury in his eyes before, but she was his daughter and she had learned much under his tutelage. She had become finely-wrought steel, her words were honed into a blade that would free her from his tyranny.

Even as she spoke, she knew he might escape the headsman. Then he would come for her with all the rage of a betrayed man.

But she was finally master of her own fate. She was free. At last.

Mary Fitzroy, née Howard, outlived her father by only three years. After her father's fall from power she lived in obscurity. She never remarried, but her legacy lived on in the form of the Devonshire Manuscript, a collection of poetry from the Tudor court that survives to this day. You can see a digital copy of it in the British Royal Archives. Both herself and Margaret Douglas were major contributors to this work.

When Kenninghall was searched by the king's men, a thorough inventory was made of everything they found. Most notable among the findings was the impoverished state of Mary Howard's rooms. It seems to imply that her father had let her fall into poverty following the death of her husband. Thomas Howard was imprisoned in the tower until the reign of Mary I, at which time he was released and reappointed to many of his offices. His son, Henry, Earl of Surrey, had not been so lucky and, partially because of his father's letter to the king, he had been executed shortly following his arrest.

I was drawn to Mary Howard's story after having researched Margaret Douglas for my other novel, *The Lady's Ambition*. At the heart of this story is a woman finding the strength to break free. In *The Lady's Defiance* I have borrowed heavily from real events and interwoven poems written by Thomas Wyatt and Henry Howard, Earl of Surrey, into the story. I must point out that I have also embellished the story and filled in the gaps where I thought I could. I hope you have enjoyed this novel as much as I have writing it.

Printed in Great Britain
by Amazon

53319639R00133